THE LAST DAYS OF PURGATORY

The Martian Apocalypse of Victorian London.

C. A. Powell

Typeset by Amnet Systems

CONTENTS

CHAPTER 1

THE APATHETIC MARTIANS

All manner of people managed to survive the great Martian apocalypse of 1898. This was done in various ways. Some, rather than run with the multitude, tried to hide and a few managed to find sanctuary of a sort. Survivors, in rural areas, had hideaways. Some, in the cities, could find cover amid the ruins and the sewers. However, many of the concealed people were found. They succumbed to blood sucking and unspeakable endings. Yet those who survived were more formidable. Natural selection quickly kicked in. The alien invaders did not realise they were on the wrong end of this biological and ecological agenda.

Martians sucked blood, their method of sustenance. Human or animal. It did not matter to them. They were indifferent, displaying an apathy to human life every bit as common as human apathy to sheep, pigs, cows and other livestock. Humans were just another form of livestock. Historians would later deduce that the Martians were planning farming programmes – the mass production of livestock, human as well as animal. That alien apathy, like that of humans, knew no boundaries.

With no fear of infection from a range of Earthly germs, the Martians took no caution, feasting on whatever their mechanical appendages scooped up. They indulged in all forms of blood-sucking consumption with ill-deserved confidence.

As a consequence, the Martian apocalypse lasted only a short time, barely one summer season. Their empire rose and fell very quickly – a weed that bloomed magnificently but died within a short period. The invaders from Mars had a few months of supreme dominance, and then the Earth fought back. The cowering humans in hiding came out of their lairs and joined the legions of germs, the rats, the dog packs and the opportunistic carrion. Humans were not like sheep.

The Martians had no fear. This was their downfall. They did not fear germs. They underestimated the boldness of the rats and dogs. The carrion and other scavengers of the sky were all regarded with indifference – an indifference that also covered humanity. The Martians began to fall victim to the various blights the Earth could heap upon the alien invaders. They failed to realise that humans had the capacity to learn and adapt very quickly.

Within months the biped Earth beings were finding ways of killing the Martians. It was no longer safe for the invaders to leave their fighting machines. But Martians could not change their ways. They were advanced and supreme. They knew of no dangers. On Mars they had clearly been absolute. Perhaps there was no such thing as predators. They were not equipped with the skills to be evasive and compete.

As the many deadly blights of Earth took toll of the Martians in their huge tripod walking machines, they died in their thousands. The mechanical contrivances groaned to a lumbering halt. The Martians within died at the controls. The carrion and rats were quick and ready to infiltrate and feast upon the abundance of decaying alien flesh. Soon the land of Britain was littered with the giant monuments of lost alien migrants. For the few Martians that remained, their existence was merely prolonged for another day soon to come. The biped humans continued to re-emerge. They found new ways to kill with a glee and enthusiasm that Martians could never have expected after their easy conquest. How could so many creatures have survived? How did they find ways to kill? What kept them going?

For humans, there were all sorts of reasons. Some were driven. Some were angry, and thirsted for vengeance. Some had faith and saints to believe in. There was always a source of motivation from somewhere.

CHAPTER 2

THE PRIORESS OF
THE SEWER SANCTUARY

Candle light flickered against the dirty brick-work of the small, gloomy alcove. An old dirty curtain cover was rudely pulled back by someone unannounced. The one little hideaway, the senior nun's one abode beneath the ground that she treasured, was being intruded upon – her little sanctuary amid the network of South London's sewers. She looked up from her make-shift desk. Her concentration was gone.

Sister Cathleen put her pen down and clasped her hands together. Then she permitted herself a minor indulgence – she sighed, and looked up. With exasperation written upon her wrinkled face, she recognised the equally formidable Sister Ciara standing before her. An eccentric middle-aged nun was staring down at her through thick, brown-rimmed spectacles with her characteristically severe expression. Sister Ciara's habit was dirty, but then so was that of the Prioress. One could not live in a sewer without getting dirty.

The Prioress had a prudent change of heart. She would never willingly cross the fiery old nun. Not before knowing of the matter they would apparently be discussing. If Sister Ciara had entered without any introduction, she had to be cross about something and would not go through the normal channels of approach. She was probably game for an ill-tempered argument. The Prioress found the stubborn old nun to be every bit as confrontational as herself when something was amiss. She would do better to indulge Sister Ciara and let her get the matter off her chest.

"Please take a seat, Sister Ciara," said the Prioress in a harsh Belfast accent. She held her open palm before her, indicating the chair for interviews.

"I would prefer to stand, Sister Cathleen," replied Sister Ciara. Her more agreeable Irish tone was that of County Mayo, in the west of Ireland. Sister Cathleen knew the spectacled nun had never suffered her as Prioress gladly. But perhaps the severe looking woman would admit that the Martian invasion, and the subsequent apocalypse of London, had brought out the best in the leading nun. The old Prioress had done well with her method of mass evasion from alien capture. She had displayed a hidden quality. Credit where it was due, Sister Ciara appeared to have developed some respect of sorts for the Prioress. Their relationship had become a begrudging reciprocation of mutual respect.

"Well then, perhaps you need to clear the air about something?" The Prioress smiled and sat back in her chair. This was something she could do without. Yet, she knew it would be easier to listen to Sister Ciara. After all, the lady was rather extraordinary. The Prioress would always concede this one point.

"It has come to my attention, Sister Cathleen, that you are to send out a number of foraging expeditions to the hospitals. These groups will be gathering medicines from such abandoned places and the derelict colleges as well."

"That is correct," Sister Ciara. "Why do you ask?"

Sister Ciara suddenly sat down. She preferred things to be her idea. Her expression was earnest.

"There are to be four expeditions to facilities on this south side of London. Nothing across the river on the north side?"

"This is correct," Sister Ciara. "Why chance the north side with the river cutting us off, when there are places to explore close to us on this side of the river? There are still some Martian fighting machines roaming the city."

Sister Ciara's stern face and the unflattering glasses lent her an austere persona. Yet she had a big heart, which people grasped after knowing her for a short time.

"Most of the hospitals would have been ransacked and cleared by now. The foraging parties will be exploring places in the hope of odd things being overlooked."

"Well, yes," agreed the Prioress. "But looking for overlooked scraps is the best we can do at the moment. The north side of the river will be no different from the south side, Sister Ciara."

"If we can better the odds, then surely an expedition would be in order." Sister Ciara replied.

"To better the odds, Sister Ciara, we would need even less Martian activity than there is now. I know most of the vile things are dying. I've heard reports that ninety per cent and more of the fighting machines are dormant, with dead Martians inside them. But that still leaves ten per cent active. Even five per cent is dangerous in the London area."

"Of course this is so, Sister Cathleen. But surely, we are at an impasse with the risk factor. With the Martians dying of this strange blight and their fighting machines just stopping everywhere, I thought we might chance an expedition onto the north side. The rogue army units and their patrols are gone as well. Most of them are dead, or they have abandoned the city. Even that awful red weed is all but gone. There is none of it left in the city now. I can only see faint patches of pink in the fields beyond the city limits. I would say that the county of Kent will be back to complete green very soon."

The Prioress frowned.

"Yes, the red weed is almost extinct. The army patrols and their shooting of looters is over. These other hindrances are gone. But there is still the odd Martian fighting machine. Enough to cause great problems. I'm just trying to explore the closest hospitals and more obvious areas to us. Some we can reach via the sewer networks. Less risk than travelling on the surface. Many factors have been taken into account, Sister Ciara. We have our problems with various types of disease, as you are aware. I have been given a list of various types of medicines to help us deal with our desperate situation. People are dying daily down here. We cannot even bury them. We have work parties wheeling out the dead and quite literally dumping them in the park areas. Without proper ceremony, God forgive us."

Sister Ciara's stern look softened. "I know and understand that, Sister Cathleen. We are experiencing many of the major illnesses. Cholera and typhus especially. What can we expect when we are forced to take sanctuary in the festering city sewers? They are the safest place from the Martians. But not from our own Earthly diseases. I'm also wondering if the Martians might be dying of the same thing as we are."

The Prioress nodded her head and took a deep breath.

"Yes, it is feasible. The Martians do suck our blood when they catch us. They are bound to have consumed cholera, typhus, smallpox and influenza. The list from infected humans must be bigger than we can imagine. Hence my reason for the raids upon hospitals, colleges and so on, Sister Ciara."

Sister Ciara smiled. "This sanctuary is fortunate to have a Prioress of Godly and most noble intention."

"Oh, please spare me the flattery, Sister Ciara," the Prioress chuckled as she held up her hand.

"The logic of your planning is admirable, Prioress." Sister Ciara raised her voice a little. She wanted to say her piece and the old Prioress relented.

"Very well, Sister Ciara," She smiled back at the determined old nun.

Sister Ciara piously acknowledged her gratification. "However, despite your admirable planning, most of the hospitals targeted for expedition have already been ransacked. I have a proposition. It is time to put this before you, Prioress of our sanctuary. I'm here to request a fifth expedition. It will consist of myself and two accomplices."

The Prioress looked concerned, but also resigned.

"Sister Ciara, I know you as a nun of a very rebellious disposition. But often you have achieved and done remarkable things. Only a few days ago, you shot a Martian out in the open."

Sister Ciara nodded her acknowledgement.

"Even for us devotees of the cloth, it was open season on shooting Martians."

"The more the merrier," agreed Sister Cathleen. She opened her desk drawer and took out two small glasses and a half-filled bottle of gin. She proceeded to pour a measure each for herself and Sister Ciara. They were nuns of the world.

"The creature had left its fighting machine, Sister Cathleen. I always take that hunter's elephant rifle with me when I go onto the surface."

"I know, Sister Ciara, and I'm sure many of us don't mind the notion of you shooting Martians. You are a nun of radical endeavour in these ungodly times. But why do you want to do this fifth expedition? I'm also presupposing that it is on the north side of the river?"

The Prioress tipped her gin back and took a deep breath. The gratifying liquid had a kick.

"It is on the north side, Sister Cathleen. This will be a surface journey from Shooters Hill to the Blackwall Tunnel."

Out of respect and a show of compliance for the Prioress, Sister Ciara tipped her shot of gin back.

If Sister Ciara was to be honest, she would have to admit that perhaps respect and compliance took second place to the rewarding kick of the liquid.

"That is a large area of the surface to cover." Sister Cathleen looked perplexed.

"It is," agreed Sister Ciara. "But most of the Martian machines are dead. They litter the entire city. From a high vantage point, one can see vast areas of London. These constructions are just standing there amid the derelict buildings. Dead and rotting, like demonic sentinels. They are now a natural part of the London landscape. I delight in the sight of them and their awful demise."

She paused for a brief smile. There was also a wicked glint in the nun's eye as she continued.

"The Martians that are still alive are unorganised. Their machines are usually isolated. They are desperate and pathetic creatures, waiting to die. One can see them from Shooter's Hill. They are lonely wanderers amid their Martian dead in a vacant city."

Sister Cathleen nodded approvingly. "So, you believe you can make such a journey with just two companions?"

"Of course, Sister. Once we get to Blackwall Tunnel, we can walk through it under the Thames. Immediately upon emerging on the north side, there is the Poplar Docker's hospital to our right as we walk up the hill upon leaving the tunnel."

Sister Cathleen shifted in her chair. "Very well, there is a hospital there. Is there anything special about this hospital in particular? There are other vicinities on the south side that we could let you explore. Would this hospital not be ransacked too?"

Sister Ciara smiled. "I anticipated that you might ask this question."

She pulled out a key from her habit and placed it on the desk. There was a look of hope in her big brown eyes peering out of her unflattering, round spectacles.

The Prioress decided to play the game. She took two rolled cigarettes from her desk drawer and offered one to Sister Ciara. She lifted an eye-brow then simply replied:

"And?"

Catching the easier mood, Sister Ciara indulged the Prioress further. She accepted the cigarette thankfully.

"It is the key to a stockroom. It was given to me by a matron working in our infirmary. This matron had worked at Poplar before the Martians came. She had done so for years. The matron said there was a young academic doctor from an Oxford college. He was based at the Poplar hospital, and he was studying various types of herbs. Things that could fight infections. The matron speaks of laudanum, which we have heard of. But then she also informs me that the young doctor experimented with other concoctions. Things in boxes and bottles that came from laboratories in Oxford and Cambridge. She said many of these things were untried. Sometimes injured dock workers volunteered to test them on cuts or wounds that might become infected."

"And these experimental medicines are in this stock room that you have the key to?"

The Prioress sighed. She struck a match and leaned across the table with a light. Her manner seemed resigned. Sister Ciara would probably go anyway, if permission was refused. The nun was always a renegade and the Martian apocalypse had intensified that radical streak in her.

"They are, Sister Cathleen." The old nun leaned forward and accepted the light. She leaned back and blew out a stream of satisfying smoke.

"I'm all ears, Sister Ciara."

The Prioress lit her own cigarette.

"There are various things and some of them could be useful against typhus and cholera. The matron spoke of concoctions of cranberry, honey compounds, something called oregano, garlic mixtures and something else called myrrh."

"My-ar?" Sister Cathleen looked perplexed.

Sister Ciara spelt it out. "M-Y-R-R-H." she was reading it from a piece of note paper. "It was good enough for one of the three kings. I have a rough

14

plan drawn up by the old matron. It says exactly where the stock room is on the first floor of the hospital and I have one of the only keys that will open it."

"Oh," laughed the Prioress. "That sort of myrrh! How clumsy of me."

"The very one," agreed Sister Ciara.

The Prioress smiled and then added. "Honey compounds? We use honey anyway."

"Well, I'm supposing that this young doctor put some type of added extra into the mixture. Perhaps enhancing the qualities of the honey compounds. I'm told that these compounds can cause germs to dry up and die."

"Very well, Sister Ciara. Who are the two companions you wish to take with you?"

Sister Ciara, hesitated. The Prioress would not be too impressed. "I would request Harry Cooper..."

"What!"

Quickly, Sister Ciara held up a finger as she took puffed on her cigarette. "He is a condemned man. A convicted murderer. He still wears prison garments. But outside, in the dangerous outdoors, we are up against Martians. Demonic beings from another world that want to kill us and drink our blood. Convicted killers make for rather useful allies. Besides, do you want him around the sewer sanctuary, Sister Cathleen?"

The Prioress was just sitting there. Her mouth open in stunned disbelief. Finally, she sighed in resignation. "My God, the gall on you Sister Ciara. It knows no limits."

Sister Ciara smiled back. The Prioress was giving begrudging consent. The next bit was going to stun the Prioress a little more. "I would also request young Samuel Hartwell."

This time there was stunned silence. The Prioress had a look of mute shock. It was several seconds before she spoke.

"Samuel Hartwell is a twelve-year-old boy, Sister Ciara. I can't possibly grant that request."

"Samuel comes from Poplar, Sister Ciara. He lived near the Docker's hospital. We are not sure if he is twelve because he is not too sure of his age. He thinks he is twelve."

"That means he could be younger." The Prioress looked aghast.

"Sammy has a few advantages for such a journey." Sister Ciara pushed the nose bridge of her glasses up. "He is a very perceptive young man."

The Prioress was astonished. "He was a scallywag and urchin that thieved. The young mite was living off of the streets. Of course he is perceptive. He targets any vulnerable looking git."

"Well there are no vulnerable looking gits left, Sister Cathleen. The Martians have had them." She peered over the rim of her spectacles. "They were among the first to get polished off."

"Polished off? Is that how we term such things? For the love of God, Sister Ciara. What use is Sammy?" The Prioress was pouring another shot of gin into each glass.

"These are exceptional and strange times, Sister Cathleen. As I have said, Sammy is a rather extraordinary young man. He knows the streets on both sides of the tunnel. He knows the hospital and that area of the East India Dock Road. The youngster is astute and he survived in the apocalyptic landscape for many weeks around Poplar and Bow districts. This was before one of our foraging parties found him and some others, seven weeks back."

"I know, Sister Ciara. But there is a reason we no longer send foraging parties to the north side. You know why too."

"Of course, but the Martians are becoming easier to evade as their numbers diminish. They are taking greater risks. They often leave their tripods, venture out with less protection. The Martians are taking more desperate chances on a daily basis. They are more vulnerable than ever. The firing squads of the army units are long gone too. We can loot and forage where we want now."

"We can't kill all the Martians. Not when the creatures remain in their machines, Sister Ciara.

And many of them do. Samuel is awful young for such a thing as this. I know the times are exceptional, but I can't agree to young Samuel doing this."

"He is better than any adult I could think of. He is from the streets. The youngster is a survivor."

Again, the Prioress looked resigned. She downed another shot of gin. "He's also a cheeky little sod, Sister Ciara."

"Well, I'll take the saucy little sod with me." Sister Ciara downed her second shot of gin with a wicked grin. She clumped the empty glass down on the desk. "He has noticed things about Martian behaviour. He seems insistent that they can read debris displacement the way a hunter reads tracks. Sammy says that a regular fighting machine that has passed a certain place for a second time will notice odd things. Even if a brick amid rubble is moved. He told me that he and his fellow street urchins used to deliberately test the machines by moving debris about. These patrolling machines would always stop to examine such disturbances. Destitute children worked these things out, Sister Cathleen. Young urchins like Sammy. Many of the survivors have learnt these odd little nuggets of information."

The Prioress sighed. "It is the odd little things that can make a difference, Sister Ciara. How will the three of you get the supplies back if you do find them?"

"We have a push barrow. One used by a flower seller. We'll wheel it all the way down Shooter's Hill towards the Blackwall Tunnel and then through it, under the river, to the north side. Load it up with medicines from the stockroom and then bring it back. I'm sure that our infirmary will find good use for these things. The matron will know how to administer them too."

"A barrow stall." Sister Cathleen smiled. "It is very obvious and simple."

"That was Sammy's idea," added Sister Ciara. "Sometimes the humbler people adapt some profound ideas. I noticed you now have the tarpaulin sheets across the tunnels. Layers of them that stopped the Martian's poisonous black smoke from getting into the sewer networks. The humbler social classes thought of that."

"The tarpaulin curtains across the tunnels were a very good idea. Several layers of them. The black smoke never got past the first layer."

"Our condemned man Harry Cooper wants to look out for more tarpaulin. He is as much a convert and believer of the innovation as he is a convert to the Catholic faith."

"Yes, I've heard of his new found belief."

"He is a little extreme in his perceptions."

"That is putting it mildly, Sister Ciara." The Prioress had a flush redness on the tip of her nose.

The stalwart old nun smiled. "Yes, Sister Cathleen. It is putting it very mildly indeed." Her cheeks were flush. There was an enthusiastic gleam in her smile.

The Prioress sighed. Then nodded agreement. She raised an eye-brow and said. "Very well, Sister Ciara, you have my permission to go on this expedition. It will be a risk, but then everything is."

Sister Ciara stood up with a big pleased smile on her old wrinkled face. She peered through the spectacles. "Thank you kindly, Sister Cathleen."

"Good luck," the Prioress replied. She shook her head in disbelief as the audacious Sister Ciara vacated the area through the dirty curtains.

CHAPTER 3

THE VIEW FROM SHOOTER'S HILL

A crisp, clear morning. London looked like Hell on Earth. The Martian invasion had destroyed the once glamorous metropolis. The central hub of Queen Victoria's empire that ruled a quarter of the planet's surface was now vanquished. Invaders from another planet had destroyed the super power. The empire's navy was useless. The Martians had descended from the sky and embarked on a rampage of destruction and killing. The City of London was dead. Nothing functioned. Almost everything, everywhere, was derelict. Now even the fighting machines had started grinding to a halt. The aliens were dead and dying in vast numbers. The city was dead in every conceivable way. Almost all the people had gone, and most of the machines were standing still. The alien occupants of these diabolical contraptions were now dead, meat for the carrion and the rats. Both humans and aliens had all but perished.

Sister Ciara looked out over the landscape from Shooters Hill, down towards the roof tops of the London district of Greenwich. Everything was still and eerie, as it had been for months, all through the summer of 1898 – June, July, August and now, September. It had been only a few weeks ago that the radical and passionate nun had stood at the same spot. She had often come here to survey the panoramic view of a wide area of London. The fighting machines had been observed as they wandered about the buildings, at first firing their heat rays and dispersing the black poisonous smoke. It had been like watching a vast factory of mechanical giants systematically destroying the human race.

But now it had all changed. The Martians were dying too. Fresh layers of eeriness upon an already eerie setting.

"You could get a better view from the chimney stack of that factory over there," said the gruff old voice of Harry Cooper.

Sister Ciara looked at the deserted brewery across the road. The big double wooden doors of the entrance were smashed open. "No need from here, Harry. The view of the London basin is fine."

"No matter how much you look out over the city, it will not change," said the old convict. He wiped a grimy hand over his dishevelled and coarse clothing – a prison uniform of faded greying blue and off-white hoops. A large letter C was at the top of his right breast with smaller numbers, 271, just below. On his left breast was the larger 117. Then came the non-regulation ammunition belt across his right shoulder to his left side. It was over the criminal uniform in which he was due to be hanged, but the Martian invasion had stopped the execution taking place. He would not remove it, though it was months since the execution date had passed. His fat, old, craggy face and his unkempt thin, grey, wispy hair gave him a most brutish appearance.

"Oh, it has changed, Harry," replied Sister Ciara softly. She adjusted the thick black-rimmed spectacles upon her severe wrinkled face. Then she twisted her wrinkled mouth in disapproval.

"Redemption must be anytime now?" Harry sounded hopeful.

Sister Ciara turned to the rudely drawn man. He sat there on a tree stump close to Sammy, the twelve-year-old street urchin. The boy was sitting on the recently acquired pushcart. It had classical sign writing along the side, *Carol's Lovely Flowers*. Rose red against a parchment background with colourful little splashes of decorative flora painted about the wording. They had a small fire going, and the three companions made up a collection of very odd characters. Nothing about them matched the normal look of human activity in a well-to-do area of Victorian suburban London.

"How many more times must I try to tell you, Harry?"

Sister Ciara looked down fondly at the big elephant gun she was holding. The ammunition belts that crisscrossed her front made for a most frightening sight. A surreal, armed, warrior nun framed against the grey sky and the apocalyptic landscape. People of the sewer sanctuary referred to her as "the mad nun with a gun." It was an ominous sight for anyone, but especially for the troubled mind of a condemned man like Harry.

"I know I was hanged, Sister Ciara. I just can't remember walking onto the platform. Nor can I remember the execution. But I know it happened. This is Purgatory. You are my Purgatory. I am near redemption. I must move on soon. God will have me. I do not think I will go to Hell. Not now."

Sister Ciara moved forward with the huge rifle and its thick, brown-leather strap. She pulled a bullet from the American ammunition belt and loaded the rifle, going through the motions of the bolt action.

"How does a nun know how to load a powerful rifle like that?" added Harry.

He had asked the same question on a number of occasions. It was all part of why he believed himself executed and dead.

Again, Sister Ciara indulged the disturbed man.

"It is the way Sir Fotheringhay Beecham taught me. I used to visit him at charity luncheons. This late and distinguished gentleman raised much for the cause of young orphans. He was a big-game hunter, and this rifle was his pride and joy. I took it from his house when the Martian tribulation came upon us. Sir Fotheringhay Beecham was already dead. This gun is of no further use to him."

"So, redemption came to him. He is no longer in Purgatory?" Harry asked.

Sister Ciara sighed. It was no use. Harry was convinced he was dead. Nuns in ammunition belts carrying elephant guns and surveying hellish landscapes all added to his troubled mind. He was a murderer condemned to hang but the hanging never occurred because Martians had fallen from the sky and stopped the execution from taking place. It was hard for Harry to take in. He was educationally challenged and a troubled man, even before the Martian apocalypse.

"Sometimes people bypass Purgatory, Harry. Perhaps Purgatory is very vast. Sir Fotheringhay might be in another part," she explained gently, trying to placate the man.

"If we bump into his nibs, he might be cross that you have his elephant gun. He might be looking for it. Nuns are not supposed to thieve things. His nibs will be cross with you, Sister Ciara."

Sammy the street urchin came to the rescue. "Stop being a prize turkey, Harry. Sister Ciara is using the rifle to kill demons from Mars."

Sister Ciara nodded her approval. "That's right, Sammy. We kill Martians, Harry. They are most ungodly beings, as you well know."

"Of course I know," replied Harry as he picked up his acquired army issue Lee-Enfield bolt-action rifle. "What else should we expect while waiting in Purgatory?"

Sister Ciara raised her eyes to the Heavens. Perhaps Harry was right. It certainly felt like Purgatory. And that was without the Martian apocalypse.

"Right then, Harry," she said in her gentle, County Mayo tone. "Have it your own way. We are all in Purgatory. I need you and we all need each other while we make our way through Purgatory. Do you agree with me on this matter, Harry?"

Harry looked hurt. "Of course I do, Sister Ciara. You brought me here. Resurrected me into Purgatory for my chance of redemption."

Sammy frowned. "Sister Ciara just unlocked your prison door. We heard you shouting in the empty prison. The place was evacuated. They left you behind Harry. The sewer people came up through the drains. Remember?"

Harry looked at the young street urchin. "You are one of Sister Ciara's orphan helpers. Her helpers are loyal. They love her very much." He looked to Sister Ciara. "I love you too, Sister. I will do your bidding because you are a holy and very righteous woman who has killed demonic Martians and helped many orphans. Blessed are these meek children. They will inherit what is left of Earth."

"So, you do think we are on Earth and not Purgatory then?" Sammy stated.

"Don't answer that!" Sister Ciara scolded. "In Heaven's name do not spoil it, Sammy. Harry is happy with Purgatory, so please do not try to confuse him."

Harry nodded his head. "Listen to Sister Ciara, you saucy little pup. You might learn something."

Sammy looked at Sister Ciara. One eye-brow was raised sternly. She expected the young rascal's compliance and support on this matter. Harry was not the most astute of men. He was educationally challenged. Sammy was uneducated but quick-witted. Although people believed Sammy to be about twelve, he was very street wise and very useful in knowing his way about the city. More so than the adult, Harry Cooper – the condemned man, who should have been hanged for the murder of a policeman who had tried to arrest him during a drunken brawl.

"This is a very strange time," continued Sister Ciara. "We are called upon for a grand mission. The three of us have a chance to do a great service to all of the orphans and other people hiding in the sewers' hospital. Our sanctuary from the Martians."

"That sewer runs below the prison where you were locked up," added Sammy.

"Enough!" rebuked Sister Ciara, fixing Sammy with a glowering look. "We are on a very important mission. Most of these Martians are dead. But there are still a few who wander the landscape. Some can still function and kill. We are going to make our way to the new Blackwall Tunnel. We will walk through it, under the River Thames and explore the old Docker's hospital in Poplar. Hopefully, there will be a multitude of medical things. We must salvage what we can for our sanctuary."

"I wondered why we needed this pushcart," Harry grumbled.

"Why not tell us all of this before leaving the sewers?" added Sammy.

Once again, Sister Ciara looked at Sammy and raised an eye-brow. "I did not want you to go telling the other children in the sanctuary. Many of the young boys would have wanted to come. They are not all as street wise as you are Sammy."

A far-off noise caught their attention. It came from across the river. They looked down at the broad view of dead London from Shooter's Hill.

"There's a live one!" Sammy called, and pointed to far off across the north side of the river. A huge Martian tripod was moving among the distant buildings and the scattered immobile fighting machines, dead Martian creations. Dead like the city, now part of the London landscape. Victims of Earth's many bacteria, Mother Earth's legions of germs. Microscopic unseen elements, that had eluded the alien aggressor's attention before their planned invasion.

Sister Ciara's jaw locked grimly as she caught sight of the gigantic alien contraption down in the London basin. She frowned contemptuously.

"Somehow, the Martian machine seems to have lost its fearsome splendour. Look at that thing wandering amid the desolation. Now, many of its fellow Martians are dead. It is a graveyard of decaying fighting machines. Alien structures that no longer function."

"They're as much a part of the dead city as everything else that is dead," replied Harry. He grinned with morbid satisfaction. "They're as dead as anything they have killed. And rightly so. God 'as passed judgement upon the vile things."

Sammy looked to the condemned man. "They aren't all dead yet Harry. That one can still do some serious damage."

"And you can give it some serious large with your opinions," Harry retorted. He was pleased with his comeback line. He thought it was rather witty.

Sister Ciara smirked and looked at Sammy. The young street urchin smiled back. "I'll let him have that one. Harry needs all the points he can get."

"You cocky little sod," Harry laughed. He had a begrudging admiration for the street urchin. He was created for this world of Purgatory.

Attention returned to the distant Martian fighting machine. They looked down at the dreadful contrivance striding about on the other side of the meandering Thames. With its colossal legs it was stepping over the wrecked buildings of the dockland area. They watched with interest as the tripod stopped before another of its kind, an immobile three-legged contraption just standing there. A forgotten monolith, rusting in the Earth's atmosphere. A murder of crows fluttered up into the sky, leaving the huge inactive mechanism, anxious to fly away from the live Martian machine's scrutiny.

"Now comes the green light," said Sammy. "The green light that can test for things."

"How do you know that?" asked Sister Ciara.

"I've seen them do it before. They let their green light shine over things. They seem to know if other things are there. I think the Martian is trying to search for other Martians that are alive inside the machines. Perhaps to rescue them."

"You are a most perceptive young man Sammy," said Sister Ciara. The street urchin noticed things. Small things and retained a sharp memory that he put to beneficial use.

"Is that good," asked the youngster.

"Of course it is, Sammy." The old nun smiled. Her faith in all things was bright and beautiful. Like the title of her favourite hymn.

Even at such a distance they could faintly hear the fighting machine's whirring as a green scanning light passed over a stationary dead tripod machine unit. The active giant three-legged machine walked around the derelict tripod. There was a definite sense of purpose as one of its many appendages held a device that glowed green. It systematically scanned the tripod wreck. Nothing of note. The green light switched off and the Martian tripod walked away towards another stationary fighting machine. It repeated the process.

"That thing is searching in vain," said Harry.

"I think the Martians are getting desperate," replied Sister Ciara. "Sammy is right. The live machine is performing some sort of check. That cabin at the top is where the actual creature is inside and working the machine. I think it is alone and without plans. The few Martians that are left must be marooned on this planet. It seems to be patrolling that section of the city. Perhaps looking for survivors."

"Also looking for people like us," added Sammy.

"People too?" Sister Ciara raised a questioning eye-brow. She always did when enquiring about certain issues.

"They need to feed, Sister," replied Sammy. "They'll do dogs and horses. I've seen them. They prefer human blood though."

Sister Ciara sighed. "Yes, you are right Sammy. I should know that too. I've seen them feed on people. They are giant leeches. Hideous and diabolical things."

The Martian's familiar call boomed out like a cow that could blow into an alpine horn for further amplification. Far off, in the distance an unseen answer from another Martian fighting machine replied. The distant bellow of acknowledgement. The lone tripod turned westward towards the central part of London. That was where the response came from. After a short interval the fighting machine bellowed another reply and began to stride away towards the inner city.

"They will not be around for much longer," added Harry as he watched the distant fighting machine walk off. "They'll die the same way as the others. They'll just stop and stand there, like stage-coaches on legs. You always know when they are gone. The carrion land on their great big heads. They can smell the dead Martians inside."

Sister Ciara's nostrils flared humorously. "Stagecoaches on legs is a rather novel way of putting it Harry." Her eyes widened with fear. "There is another coming from the south. It is heading this way." She pointed over the roof tops.

Harry and Sammy turned. Sister Ciara was right. Another Martian was approaching Shooters Hill from the southeast. Instinctively, Sammy threw a small pail of water over the fire. All three immediately took cover, scampering into one of the many derelict houses. The front door was already ajar – no doubt explored by past army patrols or looters. They stopped in the hallway.

"That is one of the smaller ones," said twelve-year-old Sammy. He pulled out his loaded revolver. "Sometimes the big ones have two Martians inside. The little ones have one. That thing is coming from Kent."

Harry glanced at the young lad's revolver and replied. "That is not going to do any good Sammy. Not up against the fighting machine. Even a small vessel with one Martian, like the one coming. Even my Lee-Enfield is not up to it. Nor Sister Ciara's big bugger-off elephant gun."

"If the daft Martian git gets out, I might be able to stick one in the thing," replied Sammy enthusiastically. "They do get cocky sometimes."

"Oh yeah," agreed Harry. "If it gets out. But it is hardly likely to do that. It is probably answering to the one on the north side of the river. The one we see calling out."

"It might see the ashes of our fire," added Sister Ciara. She was looking at the smouldering embers back out by their push cart. "It will know if the smouldering ashes are recent. They always explore such things."

"If it notices the ashes, it will stop to look. I think it will get out," added Sammy. "We should split up and do the normal thing."

"All right," agreed Sister Ciara. "Sammy, you remain here. I'll take the brewery factory. This time height will have the advantage in this immediate area. Harry, you go lower. We keep the smouldering fire ashes within sight at all times. That is our bait. If the Martian does get out, don't start blazing away, Sammy. Remain calm and watch. Just watch!"

Sammy looked disappointed. "I knew you were going to say that."

"Do as you are told, Sammy, or I will send you back to the sanctuary. Do you understand me? Remember, lad." She patted her elephant gun, looking like some surreal religious warrior. The nation's new Boadicea. "I have the big bugger-off gun and I know how to use it, lad."

"Yes, Sister Ciara," he replied. The old nun meant what she said. The young street urchin knew how far he could push her. He would comply with her instruction.

Sister Ciara and Harry went back to the entrance. They lingered briefly at the open door, checking the terrain. The distant approach of the Martian fighting machine could be heard. It was growing louder. A quick nod to each other and they left the derelict house, the nun going one way while the reprieved prisoner went the other, each armed with their rifles.

Sammy remained. His revolver was at the ready. If the Martian creature left the fighting machine and came into the house, it would be a different story. He was certain Sister Ciara would not mind him shooting the alien then. The youngster sighed. He went into the front room of the house and crouched by the broken window. He would have to be content to observe if the fighting machine spotted the embers. He had noticed the machines home in on heat. Especially if it was in the open. The Martians would know that heat was often a human source. That is why the survivors sheltered in the sewers. They could have fires out of sight. It had been so for months. The nuns and their gathering of orphans had built their sanctuary in the sewers. Many people now lived in the sewers with them.

The Martians had not paid too much attention to the sewers. Perhaps they did not like sewers.

The huge footsteps of the fighting machine grew louder. It would want the height of Shooter's Hill to survey the city. It was a good vantage point for Martians as well as humans.

Sammy grinned and muttered to himself. "Of course you'll come here for the view."

He pulled the hammer of the revolver back and locked it. From the broken window, he had clear vision of the smoking embers. They were all but gone, but he was sure the fighting machine would still detect that the heat source was recent. He looked behind him and knew he had many escape routes via the back gardens and neighbouring houses. The tripod with its appendages would not get him. He could evade them. Perhaps his confidence was ill-deserved but it had got him through the worst of the apocalyptic catastrophe.

Upon leaving the derelict house, Sister Ciara strode across the cobbled street towards the large broken wooden doors of the derelict brewery. Her black hood and garments fluttered in the breeze. Her crisscross ammunition belt shone in the morning sun and her powerful hunting rifle was primed and ready to deliver a projectile powerful enough to bring down an elephant. Why design a gun to kill such wonderful creatures? She crossed herself, telling God she would put the weapon to better use. The rifle would be used to kill Martians. Only Martians!

As she entered the gates of the abandon complex, Sister Ciara surveyed the yard for points of advantage and sighed enthusiastically. A modest establishment, with a formidable chimney stack. Immediately, the warrior nun saw her vantage point next to the towering smokestack. There was a gantry running along the perimeter wall. Like the battlements of a castle. The thought made her smile. Also, there was a higher gantry midway up the brick chimney that circled the assembly. The letters from the top of the stack down read *Peterson's*. The name of the beer. It was not one that Sister Ciara was familiar with, but then she rarely drank beer. Her tastes were more for a drop of gin or a cherry-brandy on special occasions.

Nimbly, she went up the metal-framed steps and moved along the gantry platform. There was a clear view over the wall. In the distance she could hear the tripod's huge strides getting closer. Crows and ravens flew up above the roof tops in panic. The fighting machine was drawing closer to them and soon its capsule would come into view over the roof tops. The machine had strode into an incline and for a moment it was out of sight. Sister Ciara's adrenalin was beginning to race. She looked up the chimney stack and decided not to use the higher gantry around the column. The platform she was now standing on would be fine. A clear downward line of fire for one of the smaller tripods. She could see the charred remains of their recent fire. The bait. Would the Martian come out of its machine to investigate? Fire meant a human source. Martians knew that.

The warrior nun grinned. She felt certain the fighting machine would stop by the blackened remains. The creature within the mechanism would step out – an alien being with three legs like the gigantic vehicle it controlled to stalk the Earth.

Back in the derelict house, Sammy was of the same opinion as Sister Ciara. The Martian would leave the fighting machine. It was a huge mechanism, but small compared to other Martian machines. There would be just one creature inside. Not like the double Martian controlled machines.

The first thundering footfall sounded and the earth shook. A long mechanical leg, resting on three splayed miniature mechanistic tripod toes. Small stabilising feelers. Sammy inspected the elongated leg, with its vein conduits coursing the strange alloy. Then the entire underneath of the capsule appeared, blocking the clear blue sky. It looked like a metallic almond nut shell, with a green porthole at the front. The undercarriage consisted of an array of green lights, terrifying and impressive at the same time. Slowly, the capsule rotated as the almond head surveyed the surroundings. Appendages twisted with the ends of each tentacle showing three small splayed fingers. The green orb of the porthole revolved directly before his line of vision.

Sammy instinctively ducked lower behind the windowsill. There was an untidy shrub providing cover in the front garden. He stared through the foliage, confident he was hidden from view and drank in the hideous sight. The misty green membrane of the machine's porthole window. Although transparent, it was not glass. He could make out the grotesque silhouette inside of the creature working the machine. The green substance of the view port was known to absorb bullets. It was thick, almost like a living thing. Once bullets became imbedded in the green jellified window, the goo was able to slowly spew the bullet back out. Then it readjusted and repaired the blemish. Sammy had seen a destroyed tripod up close. An artillery shell had gone through the porthole. The power of the shell was too strong – it had penetrated, and gone right through. The explosion had blown the jellified liquid out and away, like an exploding sack of mucus.

Sammy knew his revolver would be of little use against the machine – only a lucky shot from a cannon might take out the tripod. But if the Martian was going to come out, it would be a different situation. The tension was almost unbearable. The street urchin felt sure the Martian was going to make that mistake. As their numbers reduced, they took more chances and made more mistakes. The Martians were doomed, but they continued to kill whenever an opportunity presented itself.

He grinned and whispered to himself: "We continue to kill and get better chances now days. Come on, you nice big fat butterbean with legs and arms. Come out to play. We'll cut some capers with you."

As though it had heard, the machine's body trunk lowered into a cradling position below the knee-like joints of the huge mechanical legs. The whole vehicle descended many yards from its original walking height. Steam hissed out as the hydraulics toned down and stopped whirring. For a moment, there was silence. Then a side compartment clicked and opened. Sammy's heart skipped a beat as the scene unfolded.

Tentacle-like appendages gripped the side of the machine's open door from the inside. These were not mechanical – they were made of living tissue. Each feeler had three long, skinny fingers. Then the gruesome Martian bulk appeared. Some might say it was like a huge potato, with three legs and a multitude of tentacles. To Sammy, it was a giant, grey butterbean – diseased, with ugly moles and other deformed growths. It had two dark-green orbs over its eyes and a central beak for a mouth – like the beak of a raptor. The green orbs were obviously shade protectors for the Martian's eyes. Almost like the sun shades that he had seen rich people wear on bygone sunny days.

"The blooming things are acting as though they are on holiday. Bloody Martian bastards," he hissed to himself.

A small contraption came out of the door. And turned into a platform that the creature stood upon. The device clicked into motion amid the sound of whining hydraulics. It swiftly lowered the alien creature to the ground.

The Martian moved off of the lift with a nimble grace that was surprising. Its three thick legs were perfectly coordinated as it walked toward the damp embers and the barrow stall. It had no feet or hooves. Each of its three thick tentacle feet were coiled like a snake. It slithered with each step, almost skating gracefully over the ground. It gave the Martian an impressive dexterity. There were four thin arm feelers, each having three slim fingers. Even smaller appendages protruded from its body mass, hanging limply like thick overgrown hair follicles.

There was a bulky alloy cylinder attached to the creature's back. It looked a little like a water boiler with small conduits running from the top to the bottom of the casing. Sammy had seen similar things in bathrooms of rich people. From the back of the bulky chamber was a flexible rimmed pipe that ran to a device in one of the Martian's three fingered hands, possibly a small heat gun. It looked like a cross between a trumpet and a blunderbuss.

For the first time, it dawned on Sammy that the fighting machines were crude images of how the Martians themselves – three legs with multiple arm appendages. This Martian looked the complete foot soldier, with weaponry and sun shades over its eyes.

The creature let its three other feelers go to work. It dropped down in a soldier-like stance, kneeling on two legs with the third on its coiled foot. This was the way humans might kneel on one leg to fire a rifle. The open barrel ray gun was held pointing to the sky in a readying posture. The alien was sifting through the embers of the dead camp fire with one tentacle, while the other two explored the push cart. The Martian seemed to be testing the area by touch, surveying the dead neighbourhood. It seemed capable of multi-tasking, at least of doing two different things at the same time. The Martian's reconnaissance and feelers were two independent acts. The butterbean body part with eyes appeared interested in the surrounding view while the appendages did their exploring by touch. One of the feelers moved to the Martians dark eye shades.

The three thin fingers lifted the green lenses up. They were on pivots, and remained up to reveal purple irises against the dirty yellow sclera and thin red veins. Its eyes looked clouded and unhealthy. As though the creature was ill.

"Oh, you little beauty," whispered Sammy. "I bet Sister Ciara has you plumb in sight. Her big bugger of a rifle will be ready to hammer one home. Well, you sure got it coming, you cocky Martian bastard."

Sammy heard the distant sound of a rifle's bolt clicking in preparation. Was it Harry or was it Sister Ciara? Then he saw the avenging nun. She was standing on the wall of the brewery, close to the brick tower. She was magnificent in her black tunic, white scapular and her large crucifix – an avenging Christian Soldier, her hooded veil fluttering in the wind. There was a wicked crisscross of ammunition belts, from each shoulder to the opposite hip, the bullets in neat rows. Finally, the formidable Austrian elephant gun, aimed down at the alien.

"Heavenly warrior," whispered Sammy, and he crossed himself.

It was just a moment, a split second when time seemed to stop. Yet Sammy observed it all with vicious glee. The Martian dithered. It was able to do multiple things, but it was not quick enough to aim its weapon. Perhaps there was a moment of fear – had Martians started to fear humans? Had they heard of the mad nun? Certainly, she had killed a Martian before.

The nun had one eye closed, the other peering at the alien creation through the lens of her thick black-rimmed spectacles and along the rifle gun sight. The globular monstrosity sat snugly in the sight of her powerful hunting rifle. There was no sign of compassion in her wrinkled face. Sister Ciara had a task before her to fulfil. With sublime indifference and well-practised ease, she squeezed the trigger. With a crack the bullet tore through the stillness of the dead city, smashing neatly between the eyes of the shocked Martian. The creature's heat-ray device went off by reflex, sending a needle of pulsating energy harmlessly into the sky. A gush of red blood and gore exploded out of the creature. The Martian crown was not like a human head. It was part of one giant body. Like an enormous butterbean. The being's three legs gave way and it collapsed into a sitting position, then toppled backwards. The clatter of the alloy backpack was like a protest, as the weight of the alien body muffled the ringing din. Its many feelers splayed out, almost comically. Humpty Dumpty fell.

"Chew on that, you bastard," whispered Sammy, gloating at the Martian's demise. He rose, then went to the hallway and out of the front door. Slowly, he made his way up the garden path with his revolver at the ready. The breeze blew the boy's unkempt brown hair. As he got to the gate, he gasped. It was a delightful sight to see the Martian lying there, with its green-orbed shades pivoted above shocked, diseased eyes. The blood shot yellow sclera around the purple irises. Frozen in shock, the lifeless eyes stared up at the blue sky. The raptor beak open.

"Almost like it was surprised," he muttered to himself, while studying the sequence of horizontal furrowed ridges. There was a ladderlike row of indentations running from the beaked mouth and stopping between the two eyes. There was a neat, red hole between the eyeballs, the point of impact where the projectile had smashed through the abomination's grille and ripped out its brain.

"Well," he gloated, "That bullet had no time to spend with you. The mad nun's shot just passed through."

Sammy looked at the splattering of blood and gore above the dead Martian's cranium. He thought of all the people he had seen die, the helpless way they had been killed by the vile smoke. Those who had been caught by the heat ray reduced in a split second to smouldering, blackened skeletons. Others had been sucked dry of their blood while still alive. The Martians deserved all manner of demise. Anything would do, just so long as they kept dying.

He looked up as the champion of the moment approached – the formidable Sister Ciara, the warrior nun. He grinned and said, "Bull's eye, Sister Ciara. You got this one smack bang in the middle!"

"We must not take pleasure in this Sammy. It is something that has to be done."

"Oh, come on, Sister," Sammy replied cheekily. He knew when to push the boundaries with the old nun. "Didn't you get the slightest feeling of pleasure?"

"Well…"

She grinned back and her nose wrinkled like a naughty young girl's. "Maybe there was a slight twinge of gratification."

Sammy giggled. Sister Ciara was a most unusual nun, but a mighty advocate for all nuns.

"Our Lady of Martian Slaying," he whispered.

"What was that?" She raised an eye-brow. "You should not be saying things like that Sammy. It is almost blasphemous."

"But we have many saints Sister Ciara," said Sammy.

"Yes, we do. You must not compare me killing these demonic things to the piety of well-meaning saints, young Sammy. We must know who we are and know our place."

The young lad looked up and smiled. "Yes, Sister Ciara."

"I'm told we cannot use the Martian hand weapon – its gun?" Sister Ciara enquired.

"No Sister," replied Sammy. "There is some sort of trigger, but it does not work for people. Only Martians can fire them."

"That is strange," replied Sister Ciara. "I heard the Prioress say that a soldier informed her of the weapon having a recognition device."

"What's a – that?" Sammy was bewildered.

Sister Ciara laughed. "Oh, it does not matter Sammy. It just means what you said. Only Martians can fire their guns."

Suddenly Harry came into view. He was dragging a long ladder with him. "I found this in one of the yards. It is one of the extendable ones. I want to take a look inside the fighting machine. I also thought we might test something with your big bugger-off rifle, Sister Ciara."

"There is a lift thing that the Martian used," said Sammy.

"We don't know how to work it."

"Maybe the lift is like the Martian gun," suggested Sammy.

Sister Ciara smiled. "A recognition device? Perhaps."

"The ladder is better," replied Harry. He looked down at the dead bulk of the Martian, pleased by the sight of the vile thing's demise. "So, you bagged another one, Sister Ciara?"

"You men have a rather vulgar way with words," replied Sister Ciara, with nonetheless a tone of humour.

"No good trying to be polite about blowing a Martian's loaf off, Sister," added Sammy. "It was a champion shot. Did you see it, Harry? The Martian did not know what hit him. Look, the things brains have been blown into the middle of next week."

"How do you know whether it is him or her?" Harry enquired.

"Let's not get into the question of Martian gender," cut in Sister Ciara. "What is it that you wish to test once you get inside the fighting machine, Harry?"

"I would like to put something in the stagecoach by that green window thing. Where these Martians work the controls. We've seen them through the misty window."

"Yes," added Sister Ciara. "And?"

Harry smiled. "And you stick a shot through the porthole and see if your elephant gun bullet can get through and hit the target. Ordinary bullets don't work. Maybe your gun with its stronger power can do the trick. He looked at her gun and the long, thick bullets in her ammunition belts. "Remember those things bring down elephants."

"Why would anyone want to kill an elephant? They are most wonderful creatures," Sister Ciara asked sadly. It was one of many things that she did not approve of. She had even said as much to Sir Fotheringhay Beecham.

"Well, your big 'chew on this' gun is being put to better use now, Sister. It's under new holy management." Sammy beamed with pleasure.

"You London folk have the strangest way with words now," replied Sister Ciara. But secretly she liked the banter of the London people. Especially among the poor. Even during the apocalypse and what Harry believed was Purgatory, they maintained their flippant humour. "I could never understand blasphemous phrases, like 'Gor Blimey' meaning 'God Blind Me'. What terrible things to say."

Harry started to pull the sliding ladders upwards. He was under the machine and had reached the ladder's maximum elevation. It just about reached the lower part of the dropped capsule.

"The stagecoach things do drop down a good few yards when they stop," muttered Harry. "And this is one of the smaller ones."

"That does not look very stable, Harry," said Sister Ciara.

"Yeah," agreed Sammy. "To go up there you need to have some arsehole, Harry."

"Hold your tongue there and show some respect now." Sister Ciara clouted the young urchin around the ear. "You'll not be using language like that."

"Ouch, Sister," Sammy yelped, rubbing his stinging ear.

The educationally challenged Harry looked back. "There's nothing wrong with my arse —"

"Will you just get up there and do whatever it is you want to do, Harry," Sister Ciara cut in abruptly. "I want to get a move on."

Harry complied. He looked up, satisfied with his positioning of the ladder. "Lucky the stagecoach bit isn't at full height. The ladder would not reach if it was."

"It is one of the small ones," added Sammy. The stinging ear was all but forgotten. He looked up into the sky. "The carrion are circling. To the crows and ravens, the whole Martian invasion is nothing more than a big feast. They do love a slice of Martian."

"Well, they are welcome to them all," agreed Harry. He was rubbing his hands together with boy-ish enthusiasm. "We need something for Sister Ciara to shoot at inside the stagecoach thing. Something we will know has been hit by a bullet."

Sister Ciara walked amid some rubble by an old work yard's gates. She lifted up a Pears' Soap advert. "This should do for the both of you," she said, a glint of humour in her eyes. "I'd like to scrub Sammy's mouth out with soap. The way Sister Patricia did when she punished you for swearing."

Sammy twisted his face into a sulk. Sister Ciara was holding an advertising panel. It was a picture of an old woman scrubbing a young urchin like

Sammy. The boy was standing before a bowl with *Pears' Soap* written on it. The old lady was cleaning the remonstrating boy's ears. At the bottom of the picture were the words, *You Dirty Boy.*

Harry started to chuckle. He could not read, but the image said it all.

"That will do nicely, Sister."

Sammy just grinned. "That reminds me of the sewer orphanage."

Sister Ciara brought the advertising board over and gave it to Harry. The gruff old man took it and began climbing the ladder.

The nun and the street urchin watched. The ladder started to wobble when Harry was midway. The old convict stopped and waited for a few seconds as the ladder steadied. Then he gathered his wits and continued to the top, just below the side entrance. Nimbly, Harry climbed onto the machine and entered.

Sammy walked to the front to observe Harry's distorted form through the green hazy porthole. "I can see him moving about inside, Sister."

Eventually, Harry emerged and quickly descended. "It's bloody weird in there. There are bone-like levers and tiny coloured lights. I've placed the board in front of the view port. If the bullet gets through the green jelly window, it will hit the board. Should you want to give it a go, Sister Ciara?"

"All right then, Harry. We will do this. I'll put a couple of shots through. Once checked and done, we must continue the journey to the Docker's hospital in Poplar. Others are relying on us."

Sister Ciara then turned and walked a few paces away from the front of the dormant and empty tripod. She took one more look at the dead Martian sprawled out over the road. A wide pull of blooded gore beneath its vile form. She sighed and reloaded the elephant gun. Raised the rifle and let loose a shot. They all heard the bullet hit the green filmed view port. There was a *thwack* and the alien green substance shimmered upon impact.

"Keep your eyes and ears peeled," said Sister Ciara. "We don't want a fighting machine creeping up on us."

"They are very big, Sister. We can see them miles off," replied Sammy with a slight note of sarcasm.

"There is no need for flippancy, young Sammy," she replied, pulling back the bolt of her rifle. She loaded another long slender bullet. Then she rammed the bolt home and lifted the rifle, took quick aim and fired. Another distinct *thwack* – the high velocity projectile hit the green jelly a second time.

"Right, there you go, Harry. Time for a quick check and then we can be off."

Harry shot up the ladder and back into the capsule, emerging seconds later with a look of total delight. The *Pears' Soap* advert was held aloft.

"Both shots got through and hit the advert sheet." He hurled the board out. It hit the floor, but did not break.

Sammy examined the two holes. One was between the old woman and the boy and the other was in the bowl. "Didn't hit the old woman or the boy," called Sammy in delight. He would have thought it a bad omen if the boy was hit.

"Well, that is something else we have learnt," replied Sister Ciara. "It may prove useful."

Harry reached the bottom of the ladder. His big, brutish face was glowing with satisfaction as he stood there in his dirty, dishevelled prison garments. Suddenly, he was alert. He crouched slightly and lifted his rifle. The bolt was pulled back and he stood ready to shoot.

Sister Ciara and Sammy jumped, each startled by the convict's reaction. He was looking back towards the gates of the brewery yard.

"It's just a mutt, Harry" Sammy relaxed. "You got me all worried then."

Sister Ciara put a restraining hand on Sammy's arm. She was looking at the scrawny dog too. "There is something wrong with that thing."

The dog seemed unsure of its footing as it slowly walked out over the cobbled roads, swaying sideways as though drunk. The beast's back haunches were about to give way, as if it was not sure if it wanted to sit or walk. The eyes were wide and frightened, almost as though they were about to pop out of its head. Upon catching sight of the three armed people, it tried to veer away in a coy and fearful manner, almost as though it was abnormally shy.

"It ain't been drinking discarded beer, 'as it?" Sammy was perplexed. "Shall I see if it wants some water?"

"No!" Both Sister Ciara and Harry replied robustly.

"Blimey, keep your shirt on," replied the young lad.

"That thing looks rabid."

"It's got something," added Harry.

Sister Ciara frowned. "Sammy, when a dog acts like that, you must remember a few things."

The youth was baffled. "What's that, Sister?"

"Don't go near it. And never try to give it water. If it has the affliction I suspect, water will frighten it. Make it panic. If it panics and bites you ..."

"I'll get rabies," concluded Sammy with a frown. "I've heard people speak of it. Rabies, I mean. Never seen it though."

"Rabies is deadly," said Harry. "There is no cure. I would not be surprised if many of the dogs have that disease now."

They watched as the scrawny mutt moved towards a house further along the street. It kept looking back at them with big frightened eyes. Its lower jaw had dropped open. White foam dripped from its teeth. It went into the battered doorway of a house.

Harry gently shook his head. "It just wants to be left alone. I should have shot it, Sister. Put the thing out of its misery."

"I think the sleeping dog should lay," said Sammy.

Sister Ciara smiled. "Yes, quite literally." She looked up at the sky realising that Sammy and Harry did not understand the pun.

Sammy walked over and took the handles of the pushcart. The youngster looked back as he lifted it. "Are we ready then?"

"Let us get to it," replied the mildly exasperated nun.

The small expedition made its way down the abandoned city road of Shooter's Hill, leaving a dead Martian for the crows and rooks. Plus another unresponsive fighting machine, adding to the multitude of dead machines that were scattered about London's landscape.

CHAPTER 4

THE JOURNEY TO THE TUNNEL

The team of three moved downhill towards Greenwich. The journey would normally take about an hour and a half. But pushing the cart and avoiding the debris would add time. There were scattered corpses – human and horse, plus abandoned wagons, carriages and omnibuses. The scale of the disaster was overwhelming for anyone who had not witnessed such devastation before. Sister Ciara and her two companions had come across such scenes many times over the past months. They still turned their heads to observe the appalling solemnity of what humanity had been reduced to. But the sight no longer overwhelmed them. The seasoned survivors accepted it with apathy.

The military dead were usually in groups around a field gun or some other form of weaponry.

They were caked in a strange black pitch – grotesque forms, like statues encased in black, gleaming resin, victims of the choking poisonous smoke. Arms were outstretched, with curled fingers. Open mouthed faces were full of torment, frozen in violent death. They were the last soldiers for whom Sister Ciara and her group afforded some respect. The good soldiers, who had tried to kill the Martian invader, were now dead against their artillery pieces.

Sister Ciara crossed herself. Harry and Sammy followed the nun's example.

"The scattered army survivors were very different from these brave men." Sister Ciara could not resist the comment.

"What made the army survivors change?" Harry was transfixed as he stared down at one dead corpse. The man had a rifle laying over his stomach. The pitch had not settled all over the dead man. The left side of his face was rotting flesh, the jaw bone showing through the dry split skin.

"The soldiers who escaped the initial battle or got away just changed. They did not leave the city," Sammy answered in response to the old convict's question. "They tried to rule the districts, but spent more time hunting survivors than they did the Martians. Everyone hid from the Martians, and we began to fight among ourselves."

Sister Ciara supported Sammy. "The army remnant became a law unto themselves. They had tried to control London. Corrupt militia groups were trying to function around the roaming fighting machines. The militia were no more than urban pirates. They did not last long. But in that short time the militia groups earned themselves a vicious reputation."

Harry nodded in agreement to the explanation he was receiving. He went closer to examine one corpse that caught his attention earlier. Part of the dead man's collar was on show, just below the rotting face. "This one with the rifle over his chest. He is wearing a Salvation Army uniform."

Sister Ciara frowned and walked over to take a closer look. "My word. So he is." She looked at some of the other petrified figures that were scattered about. "Perhaps others were Salvation Army too."

"Things must have got desperate," added Harry.

"Like things are not so desperate now." Sister Ciara raised an eye-brow.

"No one can pull the wool over your eyes Harry," laughed Sammy.

Harry looked perplexed. His chin began to twitch. He wanted to say something but was unsure. "What's that supposed to mean?"

"He is being kind, Harry. Perhaps a tad sarcastic, but it's a compliment." Sister Ciara looked to the street urchin and added. "Of sorts."

Even amid this apocalyptic scene there was the odd play of camaraderie. The old nun admired this silly little self-indulgence of the London boy. He always pushed the boundaries. He may be a very cheeky little sod, but he had a calming way.

Other dead people were mere blackened skeletons, a sign of the consuming Martian heat ray. The engulfing energy glow stripped a person of clothes and flesh in a fraction of a second. It was more merciful than most of the Martian deaths. No victim knew much about being hit by the heat ray. All that remained was the blackened bones of a human or other animal. All in a fraction of a second. No time to scream. No time to be aware.

Finally, something of the mayhem caught Sammy's attention. Two corpses in skeletal form. Clean unburnt bones in civilian clothes. They were laying by a wall that was riddled with bullet holes.

"A man and a woman," said Sammy. He had stopped the cart to look at them. "They were put up against the wall and shot."

"Presumably by an army firing squad." Sister Ciara had a look of disgust.

"They were probably looting after the evacuation." Harry had a tone that suggested it was the way of things.

"They were doing exactly the same thing as we are." Sammy sounded bitter. "Bloody army became a law unto themselves."

"I don't think the Sally army would help with this." Harry said confidently.

"No, Harry," agreed Sister Ciara. "Your Sally army would not do this."

"Right again. No one makes a monkey's arse out of you, Harry." Sammy grinned.

"And no one flogs a joke to death like you, Sammy." Sister Ciara's placid smile contained a hint of something extra. Sammy decided to reel in the flippant remarks for a while. The matriarch had made the order via her smile that was coupled with a stern glare.

"None of the bastard soldier boys left now," added Harry. "I shot me a couple a few weeks back."

"Well, a condemned man has nothing to lose," said Sammy. "One minute they are brave. Like the poor men here. The next, they become rotten. Like the ones who started shooting looters."

Sister Ciara was transfixed by the dead man and lady. She had deep sympathy for the deceased couple. "They were probably married. Trying to hide and survive. This dreadful event happened after the evacuation."

Sammy nodded and sighed. "Looks like the work of the rogue militias all right. I remember the sods that tried to run Poplar and Bow. They got fumigated in a church where they had set up a base camp. Two fighting machines caught them in the building. We were watching from the railway lines. We knew it would happen because the soldiers were discarding their own personal rubbish among the debris. A cigarette packet here, or there a beer bottle. The regular fighting machine patrols would notice the difference. They always do. We would have told them of this, but we could not take the chance. The army would never listen. Probably get ourselves shot trying. So, we just waited for the Martians to come. Most of the soldiers must have choked in the church, but a few staggered out. The heat ray finished them off."

"The price of not being united," muttered Sister Ciara, looking down at the rotting forms of the executed man and woman.

"I bet you did not shed too many tears for them," suggested Harry.

Sammy sighed. "Not really, but then it was not good either. I remember we felt a little relieved. We could at least forage and search amid the ruins without fear of being shot by army firing squads."

Sister Ciara turned away from the two skeletons. She walked to the pushcart and looked back. "Everything broke down within weeks. The change was fast and furious. The militias came quickly and went even quicker. Let us be away from this. We must get to the tunnel, and I'm afraid to say the rest of the way will be just as dreadful."

Sammy and Charlie obeyed. They went to the cart and were soon pushing it again. The small expedition kept their nervous eyes primed. Live Martian tripods did move among the rotting structures of the alien dead. But they could always be seen from miles away. The giant rotting monuments around them were high up. Taller than the tallest buildings. And, like buildings, the Martian structures were empty. Empty of anything living. The group had quickly learnt to accept these scattered monuments. In the new apocalyptic age, the edifices of Mars were part of the natural environment. Only the crows and ravens seemed to have any interest. The Martian titans were like the deserted buildings. They were less impressive than the scattered human dead because they were conveniently out of the way – high up in the air.

The carrion flying around the outlandish and imposing monuments lent calm. If scavengers were at the capsule of the high alien structure, the machine was dysfunctional. The Martians inside were dead. The rotting meat attracted the flying freeloaders – giant food stores containing the rotting corpses of Martians. Carrion were the tell-tale sign that surviving human foragers took comfort from.

It was becoming easier to move through London now. There were still some dangers, but these were nothing compared to the height of the Martian invasion. This was the final end game for the extra-terrestrials. Their days were all but numbered. The rot had set in, but the human survivors still had to fight to live. Medical supplies had to be reached some way.

CHAPTER 5

GREENWICH

As the trio got closer to the Blackwall Tunnel, they became more alarmed by the sights of London's destruction. This was getting up close, no longer viewing from a distance.

Sammy and Harry pushed the flower stall over the cobbled road while Sister Ciara continued to walk a few paces ahead. Her rifle was loaded and ready. The nun's habit against the rifle and ammunition belts added to the weird feel of the post-apocalyptic world. Her black headpiece and long tunic were flapping with the unnerving gusts of air. They pressed on ahead into the uncanny domain regardless of their fear. They moved out of an area where only dead, sterile things remained, into an area where more dead and sterile things waited.

Sister Ciara paused as they rounded a turn in the road. She looked back at Sammy and Harry, and they brought their cart to a halt. They surveyed the new scene before them in awed wonder.

A colossal Martian tripod was sprawled across the final approach to the Blackwall Tunnel. The gigantic contraption's three upper elongated legs were laying across the main road. The dead fighting machine must have fallen some time ago, possibly a week or more. The lower legs and the mini-tripod feet stabilisers had smashed through a deserted home, like a huge blunt carving knife through a stiff iced cake. The body trunk was on the other side of the road. It lay through a shop front window and had taken out most of the floor above. The body trunk's green porthole viewer was facing the sky. The huge machine had reeled over to smash down upon its rear casing. The crows and rooks had long ago pecked their way past the green transparent tissue of the porthole. They had gained access into the dormant machine. No doubt, the accommodating mechanism's Martian occupant was being gradually consumed by flapping black scavengers. The airborne vermin squawked excitedly around the opening they had made. How gorgeously hideous the crows were. More so than the unseen dead Martians they had begun feasting upon.

Another machine was standing motionless a few blocks further off. This decrepit titan was littered against the clear blue sky. A distant Martian call fanned out across the city. It was like an evil serenade to the dead and sterile monument of evil. More carrion were squawking and flying about the lofty trunk. This machine had halted and stopped functioning in a standing position. Most of the Martian machines did. All were now part of the apocalypse of Queen Victoria's new London. An empire's vanquished soul was rotting in its past arrogance with an array of immense, festering interlopers for garnish.

Sister Ciara took a deep breath and pointed to the fallen machine's trunk. "We can get past by going under the upper joints of the machine. Where they connect to the body capsule."

"Let's get to it then," muttered Harry. "Though I am not mightily keen on going near that thing."

Sammy looked surprised. "You just climbed inside one. Back up the hill. How can you get worried now?"

Harry looked indignant. "I knew the blooming thing was dead, didn't I? Sister Ciara plugged the Martian when it came out. I know this larger machine 'as toppled over and most likely been lying about for days. It is a two-Martian machine. You never know. One might still be alive inside."

"It's extremely unlikely, Harry," replied Sister Ciara soothingly.

"Yeah, Harry," added Sammy in a tormenting manner. "You're supposed to be a big, hairy-arsed geezer. Not some big girl's blouse."

Harry's thick eye-brows raised and he pointed a finger at the young rascal. "There's nothing hairy about my —"

"All right now, boys," Sister Ciara cut in. She sniggered slightly. "Take no notice of the urchin, Harry. As you know, he is often getting his mouth washed out with soap."

Harry laughed. "Yeah, I know. Let's his cake hole run free all the time."

He and Sammy lifted the big barrow stall and pushed on, rumbling the wheeled kiosk forward for the last long stretch of road, the final part of the journey to the tunnel. They passed under the collapsed machine's legs and continued.

Proceeding along the main road, each tried to concentrate on the journey and not to look at the diabolical mayhem about them. For much of the time this was accomplished. But when they came to the tunnel's approach, there was another sight of shattering horror. All manner of scattered wagons and carts lay before the tunnel entrance. The cavalcade and the entire advance were smothered in the murky Martian residue. Ruined corpses were in abundance. Their black burnished figures had solidified, making for a most disturbing sight. It was obvious the dead had been withered in agony during their final moments. Stiffened corpses were locked in petrified agony, twisted fingers on arms that had been thrashing in vain.

"That horrid Martian stain!" Sister Ciara exclaimed.

"Their poisonous soot has blighted everything," agreed Harry.

"Don't think we'll ever moan about the old pea soup again," muttered the youngster flippantly as he pushed the handcart.

"Don't be disrespectful, Sammy," scolded the nun.

Harry looked perplexed. "They were caught here. Out in the open. They had almost made it to the tunnel. They would have been safe under the Thames."

"The tunnel would not have saved them," interjected Sammy.

"What makes you say such a thing, young man," asked Sister Ciara.

"I've been through here before, Sister," he answered. "Back in July when we came through from Bow. Did no one tell you of the tunnel before? Many of your foraging groups came through the tunnel. That is how I discovered your orphanage in the sewers. One of your small groups came upon us and we were invited to join."

"I knew you were found on the north side of the river. Many have been. I also knew that there was an unholy amount of bodies. But not like this." Sister Ciara shook her head in disbelief.

"Wait until you enter the tunnel, Sister. It is much worse," replied Sammy nervously. "I've been through it before and I know the north side area very well. I think that is why they let me come with you and Harry."

"Are you saying there are dead inside the tunnel?" Sister Ciara looked concerned.

"Yes, Sister," he replied. "There are thousands. All caked in that black stuff. The poisonous smoke was poured in from both entrances. This is the Blackwall Tunnel Massacre. Trouble is there are so many massacres that we lose count of them."

"The Blackwall Tunnel Massacre," muttered Sister Ciara in disbelief. "You are right, Sammy. I've heard of so many massacres. I did not picture the immensity of this."

"I think you may still not have, Sister. But we must get through to the other side of the tunnel. The black stuff is everywhere. The walls, the ceiling and the floor. Everything and everyone smothered." He pulled out a cotton pouch from his pocket. It contained a lump of black coal. To the front of the pushcart was a small pail of water. Much of it had slopped out over the bumpy roads, but there was enough left to soak the cotton pouch and the black coal within. He dipped his makeshift mask in and then tied the strings around his neck.

"Don't be losing the duffel bags," said Sister Ciara. "We need them for the medicine stockroom when we enter the hospital."

"They are firmly in place, Sister," replied Harry.

Sister Ciara looked resigned. She pulled out her own coal mask in its cotton pouch and walked towards the small water pale on the pushcart. She looked to Harry, and said. "You must wear yours too, Harry."

The old prisoner had a small satchel. He retrieved his coal mask. Then he went to the cart and dipped his coal into the water.

"We probably will not need them," mumbled Sammy through his face mask. "But it is best to be on the safe side."

"I agree with you, Sammy," Sister Ciara raised the damp face mask over her nose and mouth. The black coal was staining through the wet white cotton. She watched Harry comply.

"Light two of the lanterns," she mumbled through her mask. "It will be dark in there."

Boldly the group moved forward. Their wheezing breath causing the masks to get blacker. Harry and Sammy carefully steered the cart around the scattered corpses.

"Someone has taken the time to clear a path through the dead people," Harry said in his gruff and now muffled tone.

"Yes, and moved the scattered wagons over to the sides of the tunnel," agreed Sister Ciara. "There is a crude path through this desolation. It must have been the foraging groups."

It was the same as they entered the tunnel. Other travellers had moved the many dead and deserted carts and carriages. All horse drawn vehicles were covered in the same dark residue inside the tunnel. It seemed more concentrated in the confined areas. The walls and ceiling of the tunnel as well. The dead had a sheen in the darkness, caused by the glow from the lanterns.

It was like a demonic art gallery filled with twisted sculpture by an artist with a tormented mind. A hideous display of screaming humanity silenced by black coating; a petrified arrangement of grotesque statues. Sammy wondered if the artist was God. Perhaps the Almighty was laughing hysterically. He imagined he could hear the demented laughter way down the dark underpass before them, the tunnel of the dead. He lowered his mask and sniffed the stale air. "No poison. Long gone."

Sister Ciara and Harry lowered their masks.

"They look as though they've been coated in ship's pitch. Like someone painted them as they were twisting and screaming," said Harry. He was clearly disturbed. "Forever Purgatory."

"We must do a fair bit of teeth gritting, Harry. Do you think you can do that? Sammy and I need you at your best." Sister Ciara's voice was calm and encouraging.

The old convict looked to the nun and smiled. "You can rely on me, Sister Ciara."

"Men, women and children. No one has been spared," Sammy commented.

Sister Ciara agreed. "The Martians kill on an industrial scale. We can only guess at how many people across the land have perished under such barbaric and horrific circumstances."

By the faint radiance of the lamps, Harry and Sammy steered the handcart along the narrow path of illuminated mayhem.

"We must keep moving, Sister," said Harry through his covered mask.

"I agree," replied Sister Ciara. "Let's not stop for anything. This is going to be extremely unpleasant. But we must see this through."

She looked to young Sammy. His eyes were wide with astonishment, despite having been through the tunnel before.

"Are you alright there, Sammy?"

He nodded his head and replied. "Yes, Sister. I can do this."

"It must have been absolutely petrifying for these poor souls," said Sister Ciara as she surveyed the lifeless chaos about the dismal tunnel of death. "What evil monstrosities these Martians are."

"People are just livestock to them, Sister Ciara." Harry was captivated by the horror of it all. "Martians have no more care for us than we do sheep or cows." He was trying to understand it, make some sense of the horror.

"These people have been exterminated like they were vermin, Harry," replied Sister Ciara. "They are not a food source. Not these people. These ones were exterminated the way we would kill rats."

"We care for rats even less than we care for our food livestock," answered the old convict. "These Martian creatures do not concern themselves with our opinions of them. We can't reason with them. We can only try to exterminate them. Treat them worse than we treat rats."

"Rats are great survivors," added Sammy.

"We must become like rats. Clever rats that can fight back." Said Sister Ciara.

"Perhaps rats would feel much aggrieved by your consideration, Sister. Are we any different from the Martians? Or are we just as bad. A rat has as much right to live as anything else does." Harry was drifting off on morbid thoughts.

"Does a rat show consideration for its food? It hunts, too," added Sammy. They were moving as they spoke. This was taking their minds off the death and destruction about them.

"It is survival of the fittest," agreed Sister Ciara. "Let us agree that Martians or rats deserve no consideration. Let us agree not to expect consideration from Martians or rats."

"Rats are strange things. They get cocky, like Martians," added Sammy. He was trying to keep his attention off the distressing scenes about him. Hundreds of dead people covered in thick black tar. There was no smell of putrefaction. There had been none when he came through the tunnel months ago. Any subject would do to take his attention from the malevolence about him.

"Perhaps they carry diseases that a Martian can't eat?" added Harry. "I wonder if they suck rat blood as well as human, dog and horse."

"A rat would be like a little sprout to a Martian," replied Sammy.

The wheels of the barrow stall rumbled over the littered pathway. Through the tunnel of death. "Germs are everywhere. Rats are not the only things that have germs. We do too. Ain't that right Sister Ciara?"

Sister Ciara led in front of the cart, her rifle at the ready. Looking behind, she saw the light from the tunnel entrance was getting smaller. They would soon round a curve in the tunnel, then the entrance light would disappear.

"Yes Sammy. Germs are in us all." But she was more concerned at the fading daylight.

Harry picked up one of the lamps and turned up the wick. The soft glow brightened. "We get the look of concern, Sister."

She smiled appreciatively. "That will do nicely, Harry."

There was a brief pause as the radiance passed over a new section of dead corpses. There were further mounds of dead human and horses, more abandoned carts and carriages. She turned her attention back to Sammy.

"This is really creepy," muttered the street boy.

Harry looked down at the lad. He raised an eyebrow and replied: "That's putting it mildly."

His big brutish face had the look of a cat that had just claimed the cream.

Sammy smiled. "Touché."

Sister Ciara smiled. "Where did you learn that word, Sammy?"

"I don't know," he answered. "I know it's French and we use it when we accept a joke is batted back at us."

Harry was grinning and nodding his head. "I'm giving him back his chestnut."

"You Londoners never cease to surprise me," Sister Ciara laughed. "I thought that Harry didn't understand your little quip earlier."

"Oh, I understood," replied Harry, his brutish face and thick eye-brows adding to his vacant yet comical look.

"But you did not respond," added Sister Ciara, still amused by the delayed comeback.

"He was waiting for the right time," said Sammy. "Stitched me up like a little kipper, didn't you, Harry?"

"Well, it was a little like looking a gift horse in the face," Harry wobbled his head in a cocky manner.

"It's in the mouth, Harry." Sammy raised his eyes and gave Harry his cheekiest grin ever. "All that nicely delivered bat-back and now you give me that one."

"Well, you have to look them in the face first, don't ya?" Harry was pathetically trying to correct himself. Humour was not one of his strong points. Unless he stumbled upon a kindly triviality by accident.

"Well, you snatched defeat from the jaws of victory," laughed Sister Ciara. "Platitudes are false masks of wisdom."

"What does that mean, Sister?" He was once again in his usual mode of thought, completely at a loss for words.

Sammy was grinning spitefully. "It means you're standing there with your hands cupped in front of you. In your cupped hands is your bum. And you can't understand how your wrinkled old buttocks got there."

"There's nothing wrong with my blooming buttoiks, mate," Harry could not pronounce the word. He looked to the superior intellect and matriarchal powers of Sister Ciara. His face was a picture of comic folly.

Sister Ciara put her hand over her mouth, trying to stop herself from laughing. "Where do you boys find these words?" She continued to chuckle and leaned against the flower stall clutching her hunting rifle. In the dismal glow and among the Hell-on-Earth scene of dead people, she laughed like she had never laughed in all of her life.

Harry's confusion fell away and he started to smile. Sammy did likewise. The old Irish nun was always a very stern and severe character. She was a well-intentioned and caring nun, but she was usually strict in her demeanour. The sight of her laughing was very uplifting to Harry and Sammy. On a pathway through mounds of dead people in a dark tunnel underground, under a river, in such a disturbing and hellish place, the uneducated duo had brought camaraderie and laughter to a mad nun who killed Martians. They grinned. They were even more pleased with themselves and they began to laugh with Sister Ciara. For her laughter was infectious. The laughter echoed along the tunnel of pitched and tortured dead. A mad Hell-on-Earth where the three survivors still moved. Still trying to live and laugh.

CHAPTER 6

THE END AND BEYOND

They endeavoured in their labour, twisting and turning the flower cart along the crude pathway through the death and destruction of Blackwall Tunnel. The dismal light guided them through the confined hellish landscape. Their laughter had died, but Sister Ciara had been awarded even stronger devotion from her two companions. Harry and Sammy were dedicated to her cause. Of this, she was sure. The little group of searchers were bonding well. With all their shortcomings and human deficiencies, each was aware of the other's capabilities. Every human has such aptitude one way or another. It just takes time to find them. Sometimes a crisis reveals competence. Sometimes an individual can inspire others to greater feats. Sister Ciara was such an individual – a wrinkled old nun in unflattering spectacles, a grim black hood and habit of her religious order and the contrasting ammunition belts and the powerful hunting rifle.

"At least we know the Martians are dying in big numbers now," Sammy observed.

The tunnel seemed never ending as they trudged between mounds of dead people and horses. There were so many horses. Sometimes their pathway was fashioned around the dead beasts. They were bigger and heavier to move.

"Knowing that the Martians can die in large numbers makes me feel better," added Harry.

Sister Ciara nodded in agreement. "There must be a multitude of diseases that Martians could acquire from sucking animal blood. They would take in germs that their bodies have never experienced. All manner of things could attack them. As we have learnt, the Martians are formidable inside their fighting machines. But outside there are unforeseen enemies. Even a common cold or flu could get through their protective armour. These germs are getting a free pass into the Martian's actual body. Our mother Earthly germs, entering their blood stream." She smiled at the thought of such devious processes.

"So, all what the army could not do is being done by tiny little creatures that we can't even see?" Sammy was thrilled by the thought. He had heard these theories. They were often discussed back in the sewer shelters. Everyone had taken courage from such encouraging speculation. He knew there had to be some truth in the rumours. After all, he had seen the Martian machines littering the landscape of London. He did not care how many times he heard the assumption of germs killing the Martians – he could listen to it all day long. It was a fine topic to indulge. Especially walking amid the claustrophobic Hell of Blackwall Tunnel's massacre. Something to take away the dreadful sight of dead people and horses. All covered in the black residue that came from the settled, poisonous black smoke. The Martian fumigation process.

They were walking through a horrendous corridor of a demonic underworld, not part of Earth's realm, and its gruesome visions. A man's pitch-black shiny face with its mouth open. The black tongue hanging out, In the process of screaming.

Everywhere the dead were doing the same thing. Twisted, thrashing, black shiny people and horses in the process of silent screaming. Dead things that screamed with no sound through open, mute mouths.

"Look at me, Sammy!" Sister Ciara was smiling at the youngster. "There's a good boy. Concentrate on Harry or me while we walk this awful tunnel. Remember, the germs of the Earth are doing their thing. God made it so. The Almighty protects his own when they are in their kingdom. God does not care for the trespass of the Martians. The Almighty does not expect us to forgive these trespassers who trespass upon us."

"So, the Lord's Prayer does not work on Martians?" Harry asked.

"Of course not, Harry. They are from a different world entirely. We do not forgive Martians, as they do not forgive us." She grinned and her white dentures gleamed in the sombre light of the oil lamps amid the morbid dead and sterile things of the dreadful tunnel.

"You make it sound like a new prayer, Sister Ciara." Harry smiled.

"Is there such a prayer?" asked Sammy. There was a glimmer of hope in the youngster's eyes.

"Oh, I would think there are prayers for most things, Sammy. Prayers come about when the need arises. Let us be honest, the arrival of the Martians was very new for us. A prayer had never been needed before."

"We need one now," replied Sammy. "A good one, Sister Ciara."

"With our germs, I think many prayers have been answered." Harry was more optimistic.

Sister Ciara lowered her stern face and smiled. She was desperate to keep their spirits up. The awful dilemma of their situation needed some diversion. Something that could will them to keep going through the dreadful display of death and carnage. "Would you not have me think one up as we make our testing journey of faith?"

"Yeah," replied Sammy. "One that we will do like the Lord's Prayer."

There was Sister Ciara in her uncanny array. A devout Roman Catholic nun with crisscross ammunition belts. Neat rows of wicked bullets and her big, Austrian made hunter's rifle. "All right then, I'll give it a try."

Harry and Sammy were pushing the grumbling cart through the path of Hell. They smiled approvingly within the aurora of the lamp and watched on.

Sister Ciara cleared her throat and began her made-up prayer.

"Our Race of people who art of Earth,
Earth be our Realm,
Where no Martian may come,
Lest by Earth they will be done,
For Earth will be no haven.
And so the Martian will be gone;
Because Earth is unforgiving of such trespasses,
As all Earth's creatures do not let aliens trespass
against us,
Lead our germ legions against Martian temptation,

To deliver us from there alien sin.
For Earth is our realm,
Full of our Earthly power and glory,
For ever and ever
Amen."

There followed a whoop of delight and approval from Harry and Sammy. Sister Ciara's impromptu prayer was marvellous.

"Very uplifting, Sister," said Harry with his gruff, grating voice. He had lowered his mask. It was no longer needed.

"That was right blooming champion, that was, Sister." Sammy had lowered his mask too. He was now beaming with delight. "We must learn it while going through this tunnel, Sister. You could teach us."

Sister Ciara beamed. "Well now, is that not a bonny idea? Should we not be learning it now? It'll take our minds off of this dreadful tribulation. A rum little ditty for a prayer."

There was unanimous approval from her two followers. And so, the group began to recite Sister Ciara's new prayer against the Martian trespassers. They said it over and over again, burning the words into the innermost recesses of their minds. It would be a prayer that Sammy told himself and his companions – he would never forget it, not as long as he lived. Sister Ciara and Harry laughed at the young lad's enthusiasm.

"And even when I'm in Heaven, I'll never forget it," he asserted.

And then they began to recite the prayer again, over and over, while steering the handcart along the dark pathway through the tunnelled carnage of the dead. The chanting of Sister Ciara's prayer continued. It saw the group through the final length of the tunnel. They continued the recite when they came around the last bend before the entrance at the north side of the river. Before them was fresh daylight.

"Poplar is ahead of us. The Docker's hospital will be to our right as we walk up the road," said Sammy. A keen spirit was filling his being. The others were able to sense the achievement, too.

"Let's hope it has not been plundered," replied Sister Ciara.

"It was hit with black smoke too," added Sammy. "I remember seeing it when we passed through back in July."

"Was that pathway in the tunnel still there back in July, or 'as it been made recently?" asked Harry.

"There was a pathway through the tunnel back then, too," answered Sammy. "I think it was made by your lot on earlier expeditions."

"Our lot?" replied Harry.

"Well, I mean you people of the sewer sanctuary."

"Then surely the previous expeditions would have searched the hospital," replied Harry.

"I don't think they did," replied Sister Ciara. "Many of the people were from the south side and they would have only explored hospitals and so forth from that side. The purpose of expeditions to this side was to look for food rations in shops. Most of our local ones had been scavenged by the time we were coming under the river."

"It was only used three times," added Sammy. "I was found on the second expedition, with a few other survivors. We had been hiding close to Bow Road station. On the third expedition, three of the five were killed by Martians. Only two got back."

"That was only last month," agreed Sister Ciara. "The fighting machines were still more active then. We underestimated the Martians and had too much confidence in the effects of the blight. Therefore, we must now remain cautious and not make the same mistake again. We have done well to get this far. Let us be vigilant at all times. Remember that Sammy knows the area better than us. You, Harry, will look out for the odd things. Those little things you seem to notice so well."

"What are odd things in a world that is all odd?" asked Sammy in his brash, cheeky manner.

"Oh, there is always something worth taking note of, young Samuel."

Harry felt pleased with himself again. He liked having something of worth against his name. It made him feel important.

"All people are good at something, young Sammy. Here in this world, you and Harry are very sought after people. Our old world, as we once knew it, is gone. Everything is unreal now," said the devout nun, pulling a long slender bullet from her ammunition belt and loading it into the hunting rifle. "I'll make sure one is in the barrel. Just in case one of those demonic sods turn up."

Harry smiled. "Now you're talking our language, Sister."

"Yes, I suppose I am."

She quickened her step and went ahead of Harry and Sammy as they continued to push the decrepit flower stall. They watched as the old nun halted at the tunnel entrance. It had taken over an hour to weave the flower stall along the crude path while reciting the made-up prayer. It had passed the time under very difficult and stressful circumstances. Now, new and perhaps equally dreadful trials awaited them.

"We've got to come back this way, too," added Sammy.

"Yum, yum," replied the old prisoner. "I'm so looking forward to that part."

"Have you been taking arsehole tablets, Harry," asked the young street urchin.

"No," he replied. "Why?"

"I was going to say they are working very well," came the saucy reply.

"But I ain't been taking air sole tablets."

"No," agreed Sammy with a big cherub smile. "Say 'night, night, to the dancing little pixies for us when you go to bed, Harry."

Harry looked confused. "What the bleeding 'ell is that meant to mean?"

Sister Ciara scolded lightly. "All right then, you lads. Come on, let's be getting a move on there. I can see the walls of the Dockers hospital. We have almost done it, lads."

Harry and Sammy quickened their pace, pushing the handcart to the end of the tunnel. The clear blue sky was welcome. But they were still out of their comfort area. Anywhere north of the river was so. Even for Sammy, after the past weeks of sanctuary in the sewer community.

Harry unslung his army rifle and with Sister Ciara they made their way up the road's slope. Sammy had placed his revolver on the front of the push cart, where he could grab it at a moment's notice. The wheels squeaked and rumbled over the road as the group moved up the littered roadway.

"Not so many dead on this side of the tunnel," whispered Harry.

"Well, there is enough to be getting disturbed with Harry," replied Sister Ciara. "It looks dreadfully impressive to me."

"I just thought the south side had more." Harry stated.

Sammy piped up. "The south side always thinks they are better than us lot on this side of the river."

"Oh, my sweet Lord," muttered they exasperated nun. "This is hardly the time or place for tribal discord. You are worse than a group of Jackeen drunks calling abuse across the River Liffey. Every city must have this problem. Let us get what medical supplies we can lay our hands on." She was looking up at two derelict tripods.

Harry and Sammy were a little in awe of the huge alien shrines too. There were the usual groupings of crows and ravens about the decaying edifices. Two were pecking at the jellified port hole of one of the fighting machine trunks.

"Is that how they get in?" asked Sammy.

He and Sister Ciara looked to Harry. "Sometimes," he answered. "The green window jelly stuff does not repair once the Martian inside is dead. I think the holes can't fix themselves anymore. Or sometimes the side doors open and the Martian is unprotected and weak. Outside in the air. That way, anything can get at them. I've seen it when we went on foraging expeditions to Charlton and Lewisham. When they are dying, the Martians sometimes try to get out of their machines. I don't know why. They just seem to do that sometimes. Once we saw a group of crows eating one that was dead by the open door. They were just pecking away at the thing, while it lay hanging out of its machine."

Sister Ciara lifted an amused eye-brow. "My poor heart bleeds for the Martians. But I don't think I'll be in a hurry to say a prayer for them."

Sammy sniggered. He enjoyed some of the nun's off-the-cuff humour and witty remarks. They reached the top of the sloping roadway and saw the old hospital. Its dank walls covered in black resin from further Martian fumigation. Huge blotches of dark render encrusted most of the walls and windows.

"There she is," said Sammy. His gaze wandered away from the hospital and along the huge convey of stationary vehicles. Each dray was standing dormant along the East India Dock Road. Some were burnt-out husks, the result of Martian heat ray. Others were covered in black resin. There were dead horses and people all about, fumigated and black. The poisonous smoke had claimed everything. The entire area had been sterilised of human life.

Another derelict tripod monstrosity was standing close to the corner, just before the road turned onto the East India Dock Road. The machine was close to the steps leading up to the pillared entrance of the hospital.

Harry had not noticed this fighting machine. He was still watching two carrion birds fighting over a green jellied scrap at the top of the other dormant tripod. Where they had just walked up tunnel's elevated road way. He was intrigued by the crows constant pecking at the green eye port.

"Mother nature doing her thing," he muttered, then turned to see that his words were wasted. None were listening. Sister Ciara had hurried off towards the hospital with Sammy pushing the flower stall after her. "Ere, wait for me," he called nervously and hastened after them.

As Sammy caught up with Sister Ciara, his flower stall rumbling over the cobbled stones, he said:

"There is a side entrance along here."

He veered off, pushing the stall down the side of the hospital. Sister Ciara stopped for a moment then decided to follow the boy. She spared a quick look up at the tall alien structure by the front doorway and decided it would be wiser to avoid getting too close. The huge contraption was unsettling, framed against the blue sky. Such sights were always unsettling, but this one in particular was more so for some strange reason. Even if the Martian inside the fighting machine was dead, something about that structure disturbed her.

Sammy put down the barrow stall by a side door and looked back to see Sister Ciara following with her hunting rifle held in readiness. He grabbed his revolver and then pointed towards a smashed in door.

"It's open," he said quietly.

There were two corpses lying along the slope, but the group did not waste any attention on them. The dead were everywhere.

Sister Ciara reached into the pushcart and pulled out two more coarse duffel bags. There were others, but Miss Marshall, the former matron, told her two such bags would suffice.

Harry had stopped following them, as his interest was captured by an overturned wagon. There were clothes and kitchen utensils scattered over the ground. The wagon's brown canvas had almost come away from the cart, clinging by one knot. He made a note of the thick tarpaulin sheets among the kitchen things. Fresh canvas, and it was not caked in black Martian residue. For a moment, he stopped to feel the thick canvas and nodded his approval. It would be of practical use.

"We'll take this back too," he muttered to himself.

As he turned to follow the others down to the side entrance, the tripod by the hospital caught his attention. He lingered to observe the immense machine. Another vacant and stationary titan, like so many littering the streets of London. What was special about this one? He could tell it was recent. He was not sure why, but he knew there was some fresh aspect about the alien contrivance. His gaze wandered up one of the great limbs. He noted the alien engineering and the strange circular joints where the legs ended before the body trunk. In his limited imagination, he envisaged the huge bellow that the fighting machines often made. The dreaded '*Arloo*' sound. As though a huge horned instrument was within the capsule. His eyes wrinkled as he scrutinised the machine's undercarriage.

Something was not right. He backed off a few steps to look up along the body, the part he often referred to as the stagecoach on legs. Then he realised. There were no carrion flying about it. The carrion always landed upon the things and started pecking the green port hole. He looked to the side part of the body trunk and gasped. The side panel was open and the small lift had been used. The machine was empty. There were no carrion because the machine was empty. The machine was not in use, because the occupants had left it unoccupied. Where were they? It was clearly a larger machine, the sort occupied by two Martians. He looked nervously along the side of the hospital where Sister Ciara and

Sammy had gone through the side entrance. The flower stall had been left there while the nun and the boy had ventured inside the hospital.

"Oh, bloody Hell," gasped Harry. He ran down towards the side entrance in pursuit. He did not dare to call. The Martians had to be in the building. He entered via the smashed door. There was all manner of shattered glass, and medical instruments upon the floor. Discarded tins and stationery too. He wanted to call, but dared not. Then he heard them, proceeding up the stairs. Harry set off in chase, taking huge bounds as he swiftly ascended the staircase. He caught up with them quickly and held up his hand while panting. Sister Ciara and Sammy turned to him and patiently waited for the old convict to catch his breath.

"The machine outside," he panted in his gruff voice. "There are no crows or ravens on it."

Sister Ciara frowned. "Well, it was very stationary. It did not look functional at all, Harry."

"That is because the side door is open and the lift has been used. Very recently. The machine is empty."

"Blimey," gasped Sammy in a hushed tone as he looked about. Suddenly his caution deepened. "That is a double bod job."

"Double bod job?" Sister Ciara looked confused.

Harry answered the question for her. "He means two Martians from that type of machine, Sister."

"Are you saying they are in here, Harry?" Sister Ciara was becoming very concerned.

"That's what he means, Sister," added Sammy, his revolver at the ready as he checked along the corridor. He looked back to them with a look of alarm. "We need to watch the empty machine. They will want to return to it. If they do, our chances of getting away will ..." he lingered as though searching for the right word.

"...diminish," Sister Ciara completed the sentence for the lad.

"I'll go back and watch the machine," said Harry. "The lad is right. The Martians will want to return. That is their lifeline. If they get in that bloody thing, our chances of getting away are lost." He held up his army rifle. "Remember, these guns work on the creatures when they are caught out in the open. You remember that with your revolver, Sammy. In this confined place the Martian is much more vulnerable."

"That does not make me feel any better, Harry. But you are right." Sammy was clearly startled by the new revelation.

Sister Ciara took a deep breath. "We will be as quick as we can, Harry. For God's sake, be very vigilant and careful."

"I will be, Sister. You and the lad do the same. No unnecessary risks. I'll find a nice hiding place outside and watch over the tripod from a hidden point. Somewhere with a nice clear shot." Then he whispered: "Watch especially for the boy, Sister. He gets a little over smug sometimes."

Sister Ciara nodded and winked at the old convict. As Harry went back down the stairs, the old nun looked about her. New fear of the Martian presence increased the anxiety inside.

She murmured: "Stay close at my side, Sammy. We must watch out for one another while searching for medicines. Keep your gun ready at all times, lad. Do you understand?"

"I will, Sister. Do we know what medicine we are looking for?" Sammy was looking along the corridor. His eyes and ears straining for any sight or sound.

"I have a list and a good general idea." She pulled out a notepad from a pocket. "I have a certain knowledge, but there are also some things here that I have not heard of. I also have a plan of this floor. There is a store room and I have been given a key to open it."

"So, that is why we chose this Docker's hospital. One of the prefects at the sewer sanctuary worked here?" Sammy was his usual astute self.

She smiled. "Indeed, Sammy. Miss Marshal was a ward sister or matron in this hospital. Among her many keys was this one. She has instructed me with all of the items and supplies we could make good use of."

"Why did Miss Marshal not want to come?"

Sister Ciara raised an eye-brow. "For a perceptive young man, you do choose your moments to become silly, young Sammy. Is this an act or do you really not know?"

"Well…" he was trying to find the right diplomatic words. But this was one of the young street urchin's failings. "She is a very fat lady."

"Yes, of course she is, Sammy. How well do you think she would adapt out here, in this ruined city with death and mayhem from sick, angry Martian machines? She barely got away from the apocalypse when it all started. Miss Marshal is of sound value in the sewer sanctuary hospital. But her size and ability are unsuited for this type of expedition."

"You could have just said she was too fat."

"Very well, young man. She is far too fat."

"That wasn't very nice, Sister Ciara," he grinned saucily.

"Oh!" she shook her head and smiled. "If you are not the limit young Sammy."

The mild joke was over. Each returned to the more dreadful aspect of their predicament. Slowly they edged their way along the first-floor corridor. Sister Ciara checked her crudely made map.

"It's just at the end of this corridor on the right," she whispered.

Sammy held up a finger and stopped. He had heard something. Sister Ciara froze. The boy's intuition and senses were very good. There was no doubt in her mind – if Sammy stopped and was concerned, it was for good reason. She held up her gun, letting him know the thing was loaded. The youngster slowly shook his head and gently patted his revolver. It was better in the confined corridor and at close range, just as effective. He spied around the corner of the corridor. Satisfied, he looked back and beckoned the nun along. They came around into the new corridor and Sister Ciara's heart leapt for joy. The very storeroom door was before them. There was dirty bed linen scattered across the hallway. She instantly kicked the sullied laundry aside. Then she retrieved her key, the one Miss Marshal had given her.

"This is the place," she whispered, putting the key into the lock. There came a gratifying sigh as the lock clicked and the door opened. "You keep watch. I know what I'm looking for." She reasoned that with the duffel bags she could just scoop everything in and get out. "I'll take the whole lot. That way I leave nothing behind."

"Yes, Sister," Sammy replied from the corridor, though his attention was fixed upon a laundry duct by a small alcove in the wall. The broad circular chute sloped upwards. There was an overturned wicker trolley next to the chute. More contents of dirty bed linen were strewn around the floor. He looked back to the chute again. He could have sworn he heard the patter of tiny feet. A distant scuffle and scrape, then it was gone. Perhaps he was allowing his imagination to run away. He doubted that a Martian would hide up a laundry chute.

There it was again! Then it stopped as though aware someone might be listening.

"Sister Ciara, there is something up the chute." He said nervously.

"What chute," came the hushed answer. She was scooping the contents from each shelf into her open duffel bags. The nun was clearly engrossed in her chore and making an awful din.

Sammy grew agitated. He could hear her bundling multitudes of boxed medicines. The clattering of the cascading things into her bags. "There is something in the laundry duct."

"How do you know what a laundry duct is?" It was a strange question, but sometimes Sammy knew things that she could not fathom. He was, after all, illiterate yet he had a good vocabulary for an uneducated youngster. Her head peered out of the door and she whispered again. "What do you know of ducts?"

"I know that chute over there is a laundry duct. I've worked in downstairs quarters before. This is just one upstairs. Sister, there are feet in the duct and they are growing louder." There was a note of panic in the youngster's voice. "There is something in the chute!"

She returned to her chore, using the last duffel bag. There was a sense of greater urgency now. Quickly she scooped the remaining boxes into the canvas holdall and pulled the lining rope taut. She had no time to check the various medical things necessary for the sewer sanctuary hospital. The medical staff back at the underground refuge could do this upon their return – if they got back. She had two full duffel bags of vital supplies. Quickly, she finished knotting the final bag's ropes. Upon completion, her eye-brows were suddenly raised in alarm. She heard Sammy lock the hammer of his gun. The lad was serious. Something was in the laundry duct.

She came out of the storage room holding two full camp-bags of medical supplies, one in each hand. Her rifle was strapped over her shoulder and hung behind. She was about to say "Let's go." But the words never came out. Instead there was a clamorous uproar from the laundry duct.

Sammy and Sister Ciara jumped back startled. A huge, horrific mass of twisting screeching fur erupted, an ugly, twisting tempest of rolling hair.

Hideous rat tails and Martian appendages crashed onto the corridor floor before them. Alien screams from a bundle of furry confusion. The vile, fleecy thing was swarming around an unrecognisable bulk of screaming Martian panic. Sammy's revolver lifted. The barrel pointed into the tempest of fur. He pulled the trigger. The shot rang out as a bullet went into the mass. Then he let loose a second shot as Sister Ciara urged him to retreat.

"Come on, Sammy, slowly back away now, lad."

Sammy cautiously moved back, the smoke rising from his revolver. Never shifting his petrified gaze from the high-pitched alien shriek from the fleece of angry rats. The squeaking swarm were tearing and gnawing at the panic-stricken Martian. Sometimes a rat was thrown away from the struggle, but it just ran back into the melee of hairy anger.

The heated swarm were like banshees from hell, biting, ripping and gouging in a frenzy of fervent collaboration. They engulfed the screaming extra-terrestrial that had intruded upon the rats' lair and excited them to a panicked frenzy.

Sister Ciara and Sammy moved slowly backwards, watching in horror as the Martian's appendages thrashed out, throwing lone rats against the wall while others poured out of the laundry chute and joined the twisting ball of whirling fur and hideous worm-like tails.

Sister Ciara and Sammy gasped in terrified awe. What a ghastly spectacle. The three-legged Martian tried to stand amid the swirling mass of rats. In vain, the staggering Martian continued to try to defend itself. It desperately picked rats from its body, which was being eaten alive. For every rat removed, two more jumped into the revolving fleece of devouring fur and incisors. The Martian's shrill screams did nothing to invoke pity. Neither from the rats nor from the mesmerised human onlookers.

The rat-clothed alien staggered on its three legs. As It crashed against the wall its tormented and agonised screams began to subside. For a moment its many tentacles started whipping the horde, but there were always more jumping back into the melee. It was a final attempt, a pathetic dying desperation, but to no avail. The alien slowly slid down the blood-smeared corridor wall. The awful squeaking of the vermin became more intense, with invigorated and greedy excitement. Their prey was claimed, the body was free for all. The Martian had given up the fight for its life.

"Quick now, Sammy," said Sister Ciara. "Let's be away from here, lad. As quick as you can now."

Sammy needed no second bidding. He grabbed one of Sister Ciara's bags and ran along the corridor, looking behind to make sure the nun was still with him. As they reached the stairwell, the sound of a shot rang out, above the excited squeal of the ravenous rats.

"That came from outside," said Sister Ciara. A second shot followed.

"I reckon that's Harry, Sister. He must be bagging himself the other Martian."

"Keep going now, Sammy, there's a good lad. I want to put as much distance behind me and those vermin as possible. I can't stand rats."

"I don't mind them if they're going to eat Martians for us, Sister. They are welcome to as many as they can get."

Harry had gone outside to the overturned wagon containing the canvas he coveted. He decided this was a good place to hide and wait for the Martians to return to their machine. He had a clear view and a good angle of shot. Anything approaching the machine from the hospital would come into a prepared line of fire. He had barely set himself up in readiness when he heard two shots from Sammy's revolver. The calamitous commotion from within the hospital was quickly in full swing and his instinct was to go back to aid Sister Ciara and Sammy. It was at that moment that he heard a crashing of someone or something in panic. It came from the front entrance. Then he saw the nimble three-legged Martian emerge from the hospital entrance and dexterously move down the stairs onto the pavement. The cylinder backpack with conduit running to its heat-ray device in the armed appendage. The Martian swayed in a motion of confusion. Many three fingered hands lingered as the body thought what to do. The grey potato-shaped bulk, with its various warts and lumpy imperfections, seemed unsure of how to proceed once it had got down the steps. It was dithering, as though concerned for another.

Harry whispered to himself as he aimed at the Martian abomination. "Oh, you little beauty. Stand still for Uncle Harry."

The grey bulk of the Martian rested snuggly in his gun sight. The creature turned again and the green bulbous eye shades seemed to look directly at Harry. The bird-like beak opened, almost as though shocked and afraid.

Harry squeezed the trigger and the rifle cracked. The bullet struck the Martian above its green lenses. A fountain of red gore erupted out of the back of the Martians upper head area. The bullet had passed straight through. The Martian dropped to a sitting position and lingered for a split second, enough time for Harry to put another shot into the alien beast. It fell back dead.

Harry quickly jumped from the wagon and ran to look over his Martian kill. He heard Sister Ciara and Sammy as they burst out of the side door of the hospital and jumped down the steps. Quickly they threw their bags on to the flower stall and began to push the cart up the hill. As they reached the top, they saw Harry standing over his dead Martian.

He was delighted to see they were both fine, though very nervous. "I heard the racket when your gun went off, boy. Have you shot one?"

"I think so," Sammy called back. "The rats have got the rest of it."

Harry looked confused. "Now what is he on about?"

"Please just follow us, Harry," replied Sister Ciara, looking back while pushing the cart vigorously. "For the love of God, run like you've never run before. There are swarms of rats and they'll strip anything to the bone."

Sammy looked back as he ran alongside Sister Ciara. "And soon, they'll be plum out of Martians." He shouted back: "Quick Harry, we've got to get back to the tunnel."

"Oh Christ," said Harry. "That fu…"

"Come on, Harry!" shouted Sister Ciara.

The nun and the boy had turned onto the sloping road that went down towards the tunnel of the blackened dead. They quickened their step, but Harry stopped to look at the tarpaulin by the overturned wagon. What of the valuable coarse material? Such canvas would protect them if more black smoke was pumped into the confined area of the sewers. It was too precious a commodity to leave. The thought had plagued him while he was waiting for the Martians to return to their machine. He quickly picked up the rolled material. It was heavy, but he managed to get it on his shoulder and quickly ran after Sister Ciara and the boy as they pushed the cart down the slope.

"What are you doing, Harry? Come on. The blooming rats might want seconds," called the cheeky young street urchin.

Harry quickened his pace and chased after them as they pushed their precious stall for all they were worth. When he had caught up, he off-loaded the roll of tarpaulin onto the cart. Each runner was desperate to be in the tunnel where the blackened dead of a hideous massacre were lying.

The distant bellow of an approaching tripod fighting machine boomed over the landscape.

"*Alargh...!*" The far-off machine called out.

"Oh Christ, there's another one coming," muttered Harry.

As Sammy and Sister Ciara entered the tunnel, Harry took the handle of the cart from Sister Ciara. The nun unslung her elephant gun and led the way deeper into the tunnel of dead. Outside, the thunderous crash of gigantic footsteps could be heard. The whirring sound of the fighting machine's heat-ray apparatus began to charge. The energy discharge screeched. All winced at the *whoosh* sound and instinctively ducked. The vicious bolt of light ripped through the London air and into the outer entrance wall. There was a thunderous explosion.

"Bloody hell!" Harry exclaimed. "That bastard thing must have seen us coming into the tunnel. Why would it fire the heat ray if it had not noticed us? Did anyone see the fighting machine? I heard it but I couldn't see the bloody thing."

Sammy turned and looked back along the tunnel. The brickwork just outside of the underpass was smouldering from the heat ray. Smouldering rubble was sprawled all over the road outside, the very place they had been only moments earlier.

"Keep going, don't look back," called Sister Ciara earnestly.

"Keep hold of these things, Sammy," said Harry, as his huge frame bent over the handle of the cart he was holding. He patted the tarpaulin roll. "I think we might need this."

"What in here?" Sammy had a look of startled horror upon his face. He looked around at the pitched black mounds of human dead. "Oh my God!"

"What are you lads talking about," hissed Sister Ciara. She was anxious to keep moving.

Sammy answered. "Harry thinks we will need the canvas covering in case of the fumigating smoke.

The Martians will know we are here. They knew all these people were here." The street urchin nodded his head towards the mounds of dead black statues.

"Let's try to get as deep into the tunnel as possible. We should see it coming." Sister Ciara looked back as they rounded the first bend. The light of the tunnel was gone. It brought a minor amount of comfort. She did not want to see what was coming.

They meandered the laden cart about the crude pathway through the carnage of dead and derelict things. Behind the approach of the unseen fighting machine grew louder. The footfalls of the giant contraption and the alien call. It was suddenly very dark. Harry chanced lighting one of the lamps. The glow instantly re-illuminated the heaped mounds of twisted dead in their blackened state.

"Oh Christ," Harry muttered. "Here we are again. When will Purgatory end?"

"When God decides Harry. We must keep moving," Sister Ciara was very anxious. She urged them onwards and all eagerly complied. They continued to jog through the tunnel for about another four to five minutes. The push cart jostling along the rough cleared pathway. It was a hard slog but the distance between them and the northern exit was getting further away. They were tiring when Sister Ciara advised them to stop for a short breather.

"Harry, let us have some water," said Sister Ciara.

The old convict complied at took the water bottle from his satchel. He handed it to Sister Ciara. She accepted the container gratefully and took one swig before handing it to Sammy.

"What's that noise?" said the boy before he could receive the flask.

They all strained to hear. A distant cacophony of squealing panic. Growing freakish alarm getting nearer.

"It's the bloody rats!" Sammy called anxiously. He was totally traumatised. "We can't out run them."

Harry ran a short way back to the bend carrying the lamp. He held the light up for a look. The glow fell upon a black cloud of fumigating smoke. It was coming along from the tunnel entrance. Martian black smoke. Before the moving soot was a wave of panic-stricken rats. A hideous swarm of vermin before the advancing black screen. Some were being claimed. Engulfed by the fumes as they fell to the advancing wall of choking poison.

"Oh, for the love of God!" Harry looked around at the dead knowing soon they could be laying among them. Then he pursed his lips and ran back to the flower cart.

"Get the canvas covering," he said. "Lay it across the cart like a tent cover and get beneath and inside."

"What about the bloody rats," Sammy shouted anxiously, while dipping his coal mask in the water bucket.

"Yes, Harry. Are the rats coming?" Sister Ciara dipped her coal mask in the water too and then stepped back for Harry to do the same.

"Yes Sister, they are coming. All Hell is coming." The brutish man began to pull the tarpaulin over the cart while Sammy did the same on the other side. "But even Hell will not stop long. Hell is on the run and we might be able to ride this out underneath the tarpaulin and with the masks on."

"Do you think it will work?" Sister Ciara was most anxious.

"It is the only thing we can try, Sister," added Sammy.

Harry was displaying remarkable control in the dire circumstances of their situation. "We must fold the canvas edge inward and sit upon it. We don't let any rat get in. They'll not linger long, trust me. They want to get to the other end of the tunnel as much as we do."

"What you mean – they are not after us?" Sister Ciara was not hopeful.

"No, Sister. They are running from a wall of black Martian smoke. The stuff the fighting machines used on these poor people. Let's get under the canvas, wear our masks and batter any rat that tries to get in. With luck we can sit this one out."

Sammy was helping pull the canvas down. "But Harry, the rats can gnaw through the canvas."

"The little shits can't afford to stay and do such a thing, Sammy. The black smoke will be upon them before they can get inside. Be quick now and this can work."

They pulled the thick canvas down either side of the flower cart. The supplies on the top were also under the cover. Then they heaved and folded the canvas inwards and sat upon it. The lamp offered a sombre light. They were barely concealed when all of Hell's demons descended. The panic-stricken rats smashed against the covering, squeaking and squealing, little bodies hitting and bouncing off. At first, the vermin desperately tried to enter, but no one inside would allow anything to violate their fragile sanctuary. It was complete insanity for a few seconds, an assault from the legion of rats. There was a petrifying initial shock, a tumult of panic and biting against the outside canvas. There was dread as each person, within the confines of the tarpaulin, wacked at any indentation, expecting a breach at any second, The probable rip as the first rat fell into the confines of the makeshift bivouac.

Then it was gone! Hushed silence combined with heart-stopping terror. The cacophony of squealing had moved on. The assault of hissing rats hitting the canvas was no more. One or two of the rodents had made a half-hearted attempts to penetrate beneath the covering. They were repelled with whacks and punches. The tension and fear within the sacking cover had been almost overwhelming. Now the silence was screaming at them. What was more unnerving? The poisonous black smoke they all knew to be outside of their confine? Or the swarm of rats?

Sammy held his knuckles, pressing the cotton-covered coal against his teeth. His revolver was on the floor. He had been about to shoot at the indentations when the panic-stricken rats hit the fabric. He feared the vile creatures gnawing at the material. Sister Ciara had firmly gripped his wrist. She was equally scared, but managed to convey the necessary moment of calm.

"Now we have the black smoke," whispered Harry.

"The rats are gone." Sister Ciara looked about the claustrophobic tent.

"Even their squeaking is lost" Harry added.

"The sound can't get through the thick cloud outside and they are running further away." Sammy sounded relieved as he took his fingers from the coal pressing against his teeth

"Make sure you keep your coal mask on," said Sister Ciara, pointing at Harry's, which he had dropped. She lifted her dirty, wet, ragged veil over her nose and mouth. Harry followed her example.

"That was over as suddenly as it began," added Sammy in a muffled tone. He was calming down.

"The rats have passed," said Harry. His covered mouth and nose made his speech equally distorted.

Sister Ciara agreed. "The panic of the rats was almost intolerable. Now we must wait for the poison smoke to diminish."

"That fleeing mass of rats must be beyond the south side entrance." Harry's eyes were bulging with fear.

"Further along the tunnel," added Sammy. "Moving quicker than the poisonous smoke."

"Now can we last the smoke?" asked Harry.

They all clasped each other's hands knowing the choking poisonous Martian vapour was settling upon the canvas outside. The dim light of the lamp illuminated the darkened stain. The buff canvas was getting darker. Would the course material hold? Would the coal masks be an adequate second line of defence?

"The sewer tarpaulin was in several curtained layers. The black smoke always stopped at the first line." Sammy was trying to be positive.

"True," Sister Ciara smiled.

"I'm going to turn the lamp off," said Harry. "It can burn the air up quicker. We will need to leave the tent or lift the canvas to get air sooner or later. We must hope the smoke thins out before we do this"

Sister Ciara spoke through her mask. "All keep down. Try to remain still. We may be here for some time."

They remained under the canvas-covered cart in silence for some time, fearful and shaking at first. But it soon became apparent that the alien smoke was being held at bay by the makeshift camp. It had been hours. Eventually, they chanced raising the canvas. It had, after all, been a fair length of time. The black soot would have surely settled. They chanced to raise the material ever so slightly. Long enough to allow air in if they needed it. They were unsure if their need for air was desperate or not. In truth, it got hot and stuffy but no one seemed to be suffocating. They would not dare to leave the sanctity of their improvised tent, but they were gradually becoming more at ease. They knew they would not suffocate. The tarpaulin covering seemed to work better than expected. Eventually, they decided to lay down, even managing some sleep. They remained concealed for hours, knowing that beyond the canvas was an area that was sterilised. Nothing would bother them for some time. And in that time the poisonous smoke could settle some more. They had nothing to lose.

CHAPTER 7

AFTERMATH

Harry lifted the canvas inwards and peered out into the tunnel. The lamp cast a dismal glow over a vision of hell. He was wearing his wet coal mask. The smoke was gone. The new poison mist had settled as a new layer of black residue. The original dead were still where they had fallen, but there was an addition: a multitude of dead rats, all in the same petrified and twisted state. Harry lowered the canvas and returned to the shrouded sanctuary beneath the covered flower stall.

"Well, it seems all right, Sister. But it might be best to wait a little longer."

"Very well, Harry. I'm sure it will not hurt to wait a little longer," she replied.

"I bet it's getting dark now. I think we slept for some time," added Sammy. The youngster had been agitated since waking.

"Well, sleeping has passed the time. But I think we will wait a little longer. We must do as Harry suggests. The longer the black smoke gets to settle, the better it is for us."

"I'm hungry," complained the boy.

"We're all hungry, lad. We'll just have to keep our chins up." He reached into his knapsack and pulled out the old army issue water bottle which he unscrewed and offered to Sammy.

The lad humbly accepted the offer. "Thanks, Harry."

Sammy was about to offer it back, but Harry smiled. "Let Sister Ciara have a drink too. We can't forget our good lady of the cloth."

Sister Ciara grinned as she accepted the water bottle. She took a swig of water and then handed the canteen back to Harry. He in turn, took a swig before putting the container back."

"Will it be dark when we get outside the tunnel?" asked Sammy.

"I would think so, young Sammy," replied the old nun.

"We will need to watch out for the dog packs. They'll be out at night. They will always try something. The job is to take out the alpha male of the pack. The others will quickly learn that our teeth are better than theirs. Keep guns loaded all the time while we are here." Harry was confident about the limitations of a canine threat.

"Martians still wander the city at night," added Sister Ciara. "They see better in the dark than we do. I think the tripod's green viewer picks up things when the Martians look through it."

"What, like penetrating the dark? An invisible light?" Sammy looked troubled.

"I'm all for waiting here until morning comes," said Harry. "At least we can see the way ahead in daylight. It will mean getting hungrier, but so will any Martian who wants to suck our blood."

Then they all heard the sound. A dog yelping in the distance, and the reply from several more.

"Well, I think you just jinxed it for us, Harry." Sammy sounded irritated.

"This is turning into a rather disappointing evening," said Sister Ciara in her unfazed manner. She was stroking the elephant gun. "I'm not sitting in here waiting for the brutes. We'll get out on top of the cart with both lamps glowing. If the pack want to square up, we'll have a nice clear shot at any dog stupid enough to try us on."

"Oh, there'll be a few, Sister. That sounds like a decent sized dog pack moving towards us. They're coming from the south side and are obviously scavenging for food." Harry checked his rifle.

Sammy's revolver was fully loaded. He had replaced the two shells he had fired in the hospital. The youngster was confused and desperately trying to control his fear. "I wonder why they would come to this place. They don't like the soot-covered bodies. They can't have smelled us. The black Martian gas would still be strong for a dog's sense of smell. I'm surprised they are chancing the tunnel."

Sister Ciara agreed. "They certainly seem interested in something. We are the only meat here. Dogs are no longer a man's best friend."

All three set up a position on the flower cart. The medical supplies in the duffel bags were stashed out of harm's way. In the radiance of their lamp lights, they waited. Guns were primed and ready. The noise of the guns could attract more Martians. The dogs would have to be confronted. But how many shots would be needed before the hungry mutts gave up?

Harry looked concerned. He was frowning as though trying to work something out. He lifted his head and his nose twitched. He smelt the very faint odour of the black smoke. It was coming from the black residue settled upon the outer cover of the tarpaulin. Then he looked back towards the northern direction of the tunnel, the way they had returned. "They can't smell us. Even I can smell the thinning black smoke. It is too thin to harm us now. It must be stronger for a dog's sense of smell."

"Well, something is attracting them," replied Sister Ciara.

"They are not interested in us, Sister." Harry was becoming more agitated. "There is something else that is attracting them. Dog packs stay away from us. They know we are always armed and can kill. Martians outside of their machines are becoming game for dog pack attention. They don't always have hand weapons. Their machines are armed, but they seem to rely on their many limbs. I don't know why, because they are not that strong. It is almost like they don't do this type of thing outside of their fighting machines. As though they made no plan for such things at all."

Sammy quickly added his opinion. "They usually run back to their machines at the slightest bit of trouble, Sister. If the Martians are in this tunnel, they are chancing a long run back to their machine. A dog pack can catch them. I reckon Harry is right. I bet two of them have come along the tunnel. The machine that squirted that black smoke. I think the Martians are from that machine."

"Yes," agreed Harry. "They might be searching for us."

"What!" Sister Ciara was baffled. "How do you know there are two Martians? Why do you think there are two?"

"If there were two fighting machines, I would guess four Martians," replied Sammy. "It could be one of the single machines. Like the one that came to Shooter's Hill, during the journey here. But I don't think one Martian would come this deep into the tunnel on its own."

Harry's gruff voice cut in. "The lad is just guessing, Sister Ciara. I think Sammy's guess is right. It was probably a Martian machine that has two of the creatures. They are the usual machines. I doubt there were more than one machine. We would have heard if another one came either side of the entrance. We knew one was approaching when we hurried into the tunnel. It fired its heat ray at us. We know it released black smoke too. Maybe the Martians are searching for us."

"They'll see the glow of the lamps," Sammy replied.

Sister Ciara's eyes widened with alarm. "Yes, the aliens will see the glow. Let's put them out."

"No, Sister," replied Harry, resting a reassuring hand on her arm.

Sammy supported the old convict. "We could put them away from this cart, but within view, Sister. We will be in darkness looking into the light. We can see whatever enters the light."

Harry grinned. "Lure the Martians and the dogs."

"Let's not waste any time, then," added Sister Ciara, fully on board with this new manner of thinking. "We must do this now!"

Harry took both lamps. "I'll place these elsewhere, Sister. You and Sammy move the cart among the dead bodies. Off of the pathway."

Sister Ciara seemed unsure. "Among the corpses? Hide there?"

"Yes, Sister," replied Sammy as he got out of the cart. "We have Martian stained black covered canvas. Among Martian stained black covered dead bodies and black covered wagons. We will stand out on the path. We must look the same as everything else."

"Mixed with the desecrated." Sister Ciara grabbed her hunter's rifle. She and Harry got off the canvas-covered push cart. The distant howling of the dogs was getting closer from the south entrance. The assumed Martians were approaching from the north opening. She took one of the hand cart's handles. "Sammy, grab the other handle. There's a good lad."

Sammy quickly complied and they gingerly pushed their valuable load among the mound of dead, blackened bodies and two blacked wagons. They turned and watched Harry. The convict was bathed in the light of the two lamps he carried. He went a few paces along the tunnel to the south. Carefully, the old felon selected an area to place one of the lamps. It cast a hazy light, illuminating the horror of a bygone massacre. Heaps of dead bodies were caught in a wave of choking panic. Now they were just part of an evil landscape of hills and dips. A physical geography of obsolete and sterile pitched flesh. Harry quickly walked back and past them. He went a few paces towards the north entrance and selected another place to plant the remaining lamp. The second glow lit the same type of horror.

He came back and stood in the new area of the hand cart. "This is a good spot," Harry whispered.

"What now?" Sammy asked. Fear was in the youngster's eyes. For someone so young, Sister Ciara thought, he was very brave. He was fighting and winning control over the anxiety within. They all were.

"Well," began Harry. "I'll watch the south lamp. The dogs will come from that direction." He looked at Sister Ciara. "I think you should watch the north lamp, Sister. If the Martians are in the tunnel, they'll come from that direction. Let them chew on one of your powerful bullets, if they dare."

"That sounds like a good plan, Harry," replied Sister Ciara. She found a vantage spot by one of the wagons and studied the solitary orange radiance of the southern lamp. "Hiding in Hell and peering out towards the light," she muttered.

"What about me," Sammy wanted a task.

"You stay by the cart," answered Harry. "Keep that gun ready. You watch Sister Ciara's back and mine. If a dog comes over the bodies, or a Martian does, shoot it. You'll need to be very watchful, young Sammy. They might try to come over these dead bodies from behind and circle us. Dogs in a pack might do this. I'm sure Martians might do too. Look out for them coming over the body mounds."

"All right, Harry. I'll sit here with my back to the cart and keep a good watch then."

Harry gripped the youngster's shoulder as he sat down by the push cart. "Well done, Sammy. We know we can rely on you, lad."

The old convict moved to a good vantage point, a clear view of his southern lamp that would give a good sight of any dog approaching.

There all three lay in waiting. All were in view of one another. No one spoke and no one moved. The sound of the dog pack grew louder. The animals seemed spooked. Yet the pack continued to get closer. Perhaps the feral mutts knew there were humans. People with guns. The masters who no longer cared for them, no longer fed them.

Sister Ciara sensed rather than saw the shape. The presence of something heightened her senses and goose pimples rose upon her arms. She caught her breath and then she gritted her teeth. Her steel resolve was kicking in. Her rifle was primed and she looked through the sight.

The hideous lump just moved into the light and was snugly in the gun sight. She studied the three thick tentacle legs that sometimes lifted and sometimes slithered. What a vulgar refinement. Adroit, like three cobras standing upright before an unseen Indian flute player and carrying a large barnacled husk on the three snake heads. From the body was a disharmony of smaller feelers. Her finger gently poised ready to squeeze past the final biting point. In that split second she noted the bird-like beak and the dark-green oval-pooled shades covering the Martian's eyes. The blemishes and huge scabs upon the giant butterbean-shaped husk. The offensive veneer of the blemished body. It was like a giant slug, on three thick slimy legs.

The sudden shot of Sammy's hand gun boomed in the close confines of the tunnel. Sister Ciara jumped with fright. An alien shriek came from above her. A different hideous monstrosity from the one she was about to shoot. It toppled over and down the mound of bodies and smashed to the floor before her. The stricken Martian had been stealthily creeping upon her position. The fat being fell like a giant egg from a children's nursery rhyme. Sammy had seen and reacted quickly. The Martian's hand weapon clattered across the blackened surface. It was fixed to the creature by an expandable flex. The three legs and four thinner appendages kicked and flayed at the base of a mound of dead bodies. Shrieking and screaming, the injured Martian unsteadily got up on three thick legs, then quickly slivered away on the coiled tentacle feet. The flex was dragging the strange hand gun along the floor as the hideous alien tried to find cover.

A thin needle of light hissed passed Sister Ciara, and she heard it fizzle through the canvas into the wood of the push cart just above Sammy's head. The boy had ducked just in time. Instinctively, Sister Ciara looked back and raised her rifle. She aimed quickly, then fired at the first Martian – the one she had originally intended to shoot. The powerful rifle boomed. The target dodged behind a mound of blackened human corpses. The second injured Martian shrieked again in terror. It was attempting to climb the mound of dead corpses from which it had fallen.

Sammy was on his chest, with his revolver pointing upwards. His shot rang out defiantly as he injured the Martian a second time. The creature jolted with the impact of the bullet. The withering, bulbous monstrosity screamed again. The gratifying smell of cordite made Sammy's nostrils flare. He was getting a taste for this.

Harry's rifle rang out, but his bullet hit the blackened mound of pitch layered dead people. The injured Martian had managed scramble away to hide above the mound of black carnage. It was still squealing from the two bullets Sammy had put into it. The other Martian was hissing and calling in some guttural form of language. Perhaps it was trying to calm its injured comrade.

Sister Ciara quickly moved to another position of cover, a split second before a thin javelin of light had hissed across the tunnel to hit the wagon's wood, close to the position she vacated.

Sammy fired in the direction of the light bolt and quickly darted for new cover. Again, his vacated position was hit by a needle-thin bolt of light. A hissing fizzle of spitting flame came from the smoking point of impact.

Harry's rifle boomed and sent a bullet in the direction of the Martian returning fire. Another fizz of the alien heat ray shot across the gloomy tunnel, hitting the corpse mound close to Harry. The old convict let loose with another shot and found new cover.

Again, the uninjured Martian revealed its bulbous form, but was forced back to cover as Sammy's revolver boomed. There were more exchanges of projectile fire from human source and further bolts of heat ray from the one uninjured Martian. The wounded one was still squawking like a deranged pig.

"That thing is not that tasty with its heat gun," muttered Sammy. His eyes were scanning everywhere.

Again, the uninjured Martian slithered and almost skated between mounds. It fired a bolt from

its heat ray but the aim was way off. Passing harmlessly over everyone. Sammy and Harry returned
shots. One bullet ricocheted close to the Martian's
coiled foot. The dust sprang and the alien screeched.

"Did that one find its mark?" Sister Ciara asked.

"I don't think so," replied Harry.

"It gave the bastard something to think about,
though," added Sammy.

Sister Ciara raised her eye-brows in disapproval.
"If Sister Patricia gets wind of your language, young
Sammy, she'll be putting that soap in your mouth
again."

"I wish she was here now, ramming it in that
blooming Martian's beak." Sammy replied.

The approaching dogs began to bark excitedly. They could hear and smell the conflict. Sister
Ciara had taken one of her prized bullets from her
ammunition belt. The faithful ritual of loading had
been completed. Now she waited patiently for the
killing shot she hoped the Martian would present
her with. Eagerly, she lay there under cover of the
mound of pitched corpses, the war-torn landscape
of the underworld they were forced to fight in.

She looked up and called to Harry. "If you can,
let the dogs pass. That Martian sod will start shooting at the pack. I might get a shot when the fiend
gives its position away."

"Right ho, Sister," replied the old convict.

The Martian that Sammy had shot continued wailing and squalling from a mound close by. Harry grimaced at the high-pitched racket and called back. "That thing will attract the attention of the pack. The other Martian will be forced to defend it."

"That works for me, Harry," replied the young street urchin. He put his hand to his mouth and called. "Give it your best shot you whingeing Martian."

All three chuckled as the injured Martian's squealing intensified. One would have thought them morbid in such a dire realm. But circumstances had left such morality behind.

Then the first dog appeared, above a mound of dead. It was an alpha male, a snarling crossbreed. Part German Shepherd and part something else. The mutt recognised the three humans. It knew what the guns could do and it went around Harry via the corpse mounds on the opposite side of the tunnel wall. The brute was giving the three humans a wide and respectful quarter. Other feral hounds followed in the alpha male's track, a collection of scrawny and snarling crossbred dogs. All were respectful of the humans in their midst.

"All yours, you greedy mutts," muttered Harry.

"Help yourselves to a nice slice of Martian," giggled Sammy.

Sister Ciara took no notice of the 'puppy-dog tails' male behaviour. She found herself a good spot as Harry came and settled close by. Sammy also crawled nearby and was ready. All three pointed their guns to a position where they expected the uninjured Martian to be hiding.

The yelping dog pack started to circle the vicinity of where the Martians were. They seemed interested in the noisy and injured one. Gradually, they made their way over the mounds of pitch dead, towards the area where the wounded Martian's moans were coming.

"Dinner time, Rover." Sammy was enjoying the moment. He looked down as he heard a scrapping upon the floor. It was the suffering Martian's hand gun. The flexed attachment was being pulled and the hidden alien was obviously trying to retrieve its weapon. It knew the dogs would be hunting it. Sammy crawled from his hiding place and grabbed the small gun. The device had a strange barrel shaped like a miniature blunderbuss of old. He looked back to Harry and Sister Ciara. He was engaged in a tug of war with the hidden Martian.

Harry came to the rescue. He cut through the flex with a sharp knife that he pulled from his belt. The loose and severed cable shot off to the hidden creature's position. The extra-terrestrial still whimpered in piteous pain. The doomed Martian now knew it was defenceless. Harry and Sammy scrambled back to their cover positions. They watched as the dog pack slowly circled the area where the injured Martian was.

The scene before them began to unfold, as a scrawny mutt ventured forwards. It peered over a mound of pitched corpses to look down at the unseen injured alien prey. Its vicious teeth were displayed in a spiteful, saliva-dripping snarl. It was about to pounce.

Then a bolt of thin light hissed across the tunnel into the fur of the mutt's chest. It yelped and somersaulted backwards. Sister Ciara's rifle boomed in the direction of the remaining unin-jured Martian, which had given itself away to fire at the mutt. The shocked alien smashed back against the wall of corpses as the high velocity projectile pierced it and ruptured out of its rear fleshy bulk. Most of its innards had been dragged out of its back. It threw the heat gun harmlessly into the air. A reflex action.

Harry's rifle cracked and so too did Sammy's revolver. The dead alien had been hit by all three different calibre bullets. It had presented itself to a ready-made firing squad. Its death was more merci-ful than the injured comrade. The grotesque form of the three-legged creature collapsed down into the usual sitting position before falling backwards. The cylindrical container on its back clanging against the hard ground.

More snarling mutts moved forward over the blackened corpses and past the dead hound of their pack, the one hit by the thin heat ray. The alpha male jumped first as the hidden injured Martian let out a further terrified scream. The snarling brute was growling, biting and snarling as the rest of the pack came over the mound of corpses into the carnage of attack. The Martian's screams abruptly stopped amid the ripping devastation of canine fury.

"I got it twice, Sister. It definitely has two bullets in its body."

Sister Ciara caught her breath. She needed to gather her confused and frightened wits. "Well done, Sammy. It also has a multitude of canine teeth inside it too." She retreated from the wagon and knelt down next to Sammy, back in the glow of the lamplight. When she looked back she could still see the dead bulk of the Martian she had just slain. They could all hear the continued devouring of the other Martian.

"So, we have got two of the vermin," she muttered, surveying the top of the corpses. "If there are any other bastards, they'll get a dose of bullets and dog teeth too."

Sammy grinned at Sister Ciara. His fear was subsiding faster now that the formidable nun was next to him. He adored this strange lady of the cloth that sometimes swore. She broke all the rules. But would not let him break any.

"Yeah, we'll get them, Sister Ciara," he said. Enthusiasm was gripping him.

In the fading light, Harry backed away from his position. "I can hear more dogs. I think the gun shots have got their ganders up." He paused and then continued excitedly. "Blimey! There is another huge brute."

He retreated from his position and came back to the handcart to kneel beside Sister Ciara and Sammy. "Our backs are to the wall and we will have clear shots at them," said Sister Ciara.

In unison, Harry and Sammy answered. "They will want the other Martian, Sister."

Sammy added. "The one we did the firing-squad job on."

"I shot it first," she raised a competitive eye-brow. There was also a hint of humour.

"We all got a slice of that one, Sister. But you got it first," laughed the youngster. The danger was not past but the mood was flippant amid the ghastly tunnel of the dead and snarling dogs.

"Are you both sure these new dogs will want the other dead Martian?" she asked, while putting a fresh round into her hunting rifle. "If they are, then I'm sure they are quite welcome to it." It was an offhand joke but her heart was beating with apprehension. The situation was tense, and each of the group needed some reassurance.

Before them, in the dim light and on the cleared path, a huge hound walked past. It looked at them briefly but showed no interest. More mongrel hounds followed. Some came over the corpses and dropped down in front of the group, but the beasts quickly scurried off, as if knowing the masters would not tolerate the pack, if provoked. The dogs knew of man's fire sticks and had a healthy respect for cornered humans. The enemies of man were different. They could be attacked outside their high homes on giant legs. They were tasty too.

They heard the growl of the second alpha male and then the excited barking of the rest of the pack. This was followed by the sound of attack as the two packs began to battle over the spoils. There was growling and frenzied biting amid the high-pitched screams of competing dogs. It was glorious to all three people as they crouched by the pushcart in their hellish sanctuary.

It was Sister Ciara who spoke first. "Let us be getting out of here now, boys. I don't want to outstay our welcome."

Harry nodded. "I think that one gets a hands-up from me, Sister."

"Me too," agreed Sammy.

"I'm rapidly coming to the conclusion that all of God's creatures hate Martians. I think they hate them more than we do."

"Well, that one works for me too, Sister," replied Sammy.

"Hands-up again for that one," added Harry.

They pushed the handcart out onto the hideous pathway. The road led through an underworld of black-coated dead. They never looked back at the glow of the northern lamp, where the frenzied growling and biting continued to add another hellish taint to the already defiled tunnel. Two Martians were dead, and a pack of hungry dogs were feeding and fighting over them.

"The Martians are up against everything," whispered Harry as they moved on along the pathway of Blackwall Tunnel. "It is not just the human race. They are being attacked by everything."

"Everything Earth-born," agreed Sister Ciara. "Every tiny germ, or animal. Human, dog and rat. It must be God's work."

"Do you think the Martians have upset God?" asked Sammy with high hopes.

"I am positive of it, young Sammy. God is on our side. He hates Martians." She smiled humorously.

Their caution was gone as far as the tunnel and its dead were concerned. There was an overwhelming desire to move quickly, to put as much distance between them and the hungry dog pack as possible. They maintained a demanding pace for at least twenty minutes. Behind them, the frenzied dog pack's feasting continued, but the sound diminished as the group moved onwards. They had not realised that the end of the tunnel was so close. They felt the cold night air first and then they realised – the end of the tunnel was imminent. Very close indeed.

"Slow down a little," instructed Sister Ciara in a hushed tone. "We will observe the outside before we push the cart out. We must remain cautious."

"Yes, Sister," agreed Harry.

Sammy nodded his head and stopped the cart. Then he whispered. "I'm not standing in here on my own, while you two go and look."

Sister Ciara smiled, though no one could see in the darkness. "Of course we will not leave you alone, Sammy. We will need to find shelter in some nearby house or other abode."

"So, we are not going to make for Shooter's Hill and our section of the sewers?" asked Harry.

"No, Harry," replied the nun. "We can't see anything in this darkness. I am also wary of dog packs at night. We can't see them. We can't see anything." There was a chill breeze sweeping down the road towards the tunnel.

"I know of an old yard close by," whispered Sammy. "We can go there until the morning."

"Well then, Sammy." Sister Ciara smiled again and this time Sammy made out her white teeth. "Lead the way, lad."

They pushed the cart out of the tunnel into the dark, cold night air. Carefully they passed the scattered debris and dead bodies, unfortunate souls who never got inside the tunnel. The night chill carried a promise of the coming autumn. They steered the cart around the carnage and mayhem up the southern slope and away from the tunnel into a dreadful dead London hidden by night. It had been a very testing time indeed. They needed to reach some sort of sanctuary. Sister Ciara and Harry were totally reliant on the twelve-year-old boy for this. The street urchin was more valuable than gold dust.

Sammy was as good as his word. In a very short space of time, they were before high wooden gates of a metal foundry yard. The huge doors were easy to push open. They quickly wheeled in their cart with its valuable cargo into the yard. Then Harry quickly closed the door behind them. For a moment they paused, to take a breather and then decide what to do next.

Sammy looked up at the night sky. There were no stars. "Must be cloudy," he muttered.

"Even if it was clear, we would no longer worry about the falling stars. There have been none for weeks." Sister Ciara replied.

Harry agreed. "That is best of all."

Sammy smiled. "No more falling stars. Not like in early summer when the Martians were shooting across the night sky. Groups of shooting lights, landing all across the country in every direction."

Sister Ciara changed the subject. "We must be able to find some lamps in this place."

"There must be a few about somewhere," replied Harry as he walked over to a side-office door. He emerged carrying a lamp and brought it over to the cart. He delved into his knapsack and pulled out some matches. In seconds he had a flame going. The foundry yard was bathed in an almost homely night glow.

"Let's get ourselves inside," suggested Sister Ciara.

Happy to comply, Sammy followed Harry, who was holding the light. They went back to the office where he found another useable lantern. Upon entering the workplace premises, they nodded approval. The place looked comfortable.

"This will make for a good stay. A nice shelter with a door for the night," said Harry.

"We'll get a good early start in the morning. First light should do nicely. We'll get up Shooter's Hill and make for the sewer entrance we started from."

"Blimey!" replied Sammy. "We're standing in money. Look!"

As they looked down at the floor, they realised that the office was littered with paper money and coinage.

"Money is no good in Purgatory," said Harry.

Sister Ciara laughed too. "What can you buy, Sammy?"

Sammy was on the floor. "There are loads of pound notes, ten bob notes and some big brazen fivers. Bloody hell. I've never seen fivers up this close."

"Sammy," said Sister Ciara a little more firmly.

The boy looked up. "Yes Sister," he replied.

"What can you buy with this money?"

He thought for a moment and then looked up. "Nothing. Nothing at all, Sister. I can just take what I want. If I can carry whatever it is I might want. I never thought of that. Money is useless. Rich and poor doesn't happen anymore."

"It does not exist," corrected Sister Ciara with a smile. "That's right, Sammy. That world of money is no longer here."

"If the Martians die, money might come back."

"Oh, I'm sure it will, young Sammy, but this old currency will be useless. Not worth the paper it is printed on."

Harry spoke up. "Might as well wipe your arse…"

"Yes, thank you Harry," cut in Sister Ciara with a big beaming smile. "Or we can have real fun and burn the stuff in the fire grating. It would keep us warm during the night, and I notice we have curtains at the office window. It will supress the glow. How would you like to burn money? Pounds and pounds of money."

Sammy grinned. So did Harry. They were like a couple of school boys who had been allowed to do something outstandingly naughty with no punishment.

"Close the curtains, Harry. Sammy, gather the notes and put them in the grating. We will extract some worth out of this paper money. A nice fire, and Harry still has some water."

"There are taps outside, Sister," said Harry.

"I'm not sure about the water, Harry. It is contaminated. We could boil some if we can find some pans."

"Shall I see of I can find some, Sister?" asked the old convict.

"Yes, I think it would be a good idea. Any sound of a fighting machine, then dowse the lamp. Even if it is far off."

Sister Ciara had found two more lanterns in the office and was lighting another for Harry to use while he searched the old abandoned establishment. "Would you bring in the medical supplies from the cart Sammy? I do not want to leave them in the open. Even though they are covered.

I think it would be best to keep them close to hand."

"Yes, Sister," replied the lad. He got up and went outside with Harry, who was equipped with his own lantern.

CHAPTER 8

THE IRON FOUNDRY

O utside, in the post-apocalyptic London night, the surviving Martians were mobile in the extreme outlying districts of the dead city. Now and then a distant call of their machines could be heard, but such calls seemed far off in the night. All that remained in South London's Greenwich area were the pathetic remnants of dead machines. They stood here and there amid the ruins, sad elevated tombs in the drizzle, rusting and rotting with decomposing alien flesh within.

In the abandoned metal foundry yard, Sammy was grinning. He had a handful of pound and some ten-shilling notes. The youngster had never held so much money. Yet it was useless now. The fire was burning and he wanted to add a little more paper as fuel. There were a number of pots simmering away, one with beans and another with water for the tea-pot. There was also some tinned corn beef. Harry's search had been rather fruitful, especially in a small kitchen area.

"Go on then," laughed the old nun with a raised eye-brow. She was putting some tea leaves into a pot. The office had kept a few amenities in a small locker. Tea was always essential in most British establishments.

"I feel a bit wicked," he giggled.

"More wickedness comes from money," said Sister Ciara. "The root of all evil."

"Yeah," agreed Harry. "That stuff and religion."

Sammy looked at the giant man. "Harry, you're about as subtle as a bucket of sick."

Sister Ciara took a deep breath and fixed Harry with a rather stern eye. "Well Harry, how are you going to explain that one to Saint Peter when asking to pass the grand gates?"

"Oh, I did not mean the one true religion, Sister." Harry was trying to make amends, much to the amusement of Sister Ciara and Sammy.

"Gaw blimey, Harry. You got your whole foot in your cake hole just then." Sammy thought the old convict was stupidly superb. The condemned man was innocent and comical without meaning to be.

Sister Ciara laughed. The comedy of the two before her was, once again, infectious. She had to grip her stomach. The mirth was so intense and she shook convulsively at the language. "Two scallywags as ever there was. You boys are too much." She continued to chuckle. Tears oozed from her eyes. "For the love of God, young Sammy. Throw the money on the fire. Let's all enjoy the spectacle."

Sammy shrugged. "As easy as it come, it goes just as easy." He threw the bank notes onto the fire and watched as it burned, devoured by crackling flames.

Sister Ciara was wiping the gleeful tears from her eyes. She also began to pour boiling water through a tea strainer into another pot. She then allowed the strained water to boil again.

"If there are any germs in the water they'll be gone after that." Harry said.

"Of course, Harry," replied Sister Ciara. "We can never be too sure. We don't want to make ourselves ill."

"Yeah," agreed Sammy. "We'll end up taking all the medicine." He put his hand into the duffel bag and pulled out a small box. "What are these ones for?"

Harry looked at the label. "Sup... sup," he looked at Sister Ciara.

"Suppository," she replied.

"What does suppository cure?" asked Sammy.

"It is a different tablet. They sometimes used them in prison. You don't swallow them. They get shoved up your jack..."

"Yes, thank you, Harry." Sister Ciara leaned over and took the box from Sammy's hand.

"Why are they like little bullet shapes?" asked the youngster innocently.

"They are tablets to put in your bum." Harry knew Sister Ciara wanted him to take a more diplomatic approach. But by the look on the nun's face, he thought he may have failed again.

"You can't take medicine up—"

"All right Sammy, I'll try to explain this to you." She fixed Harry with a look that implored he be quiet.

"Some of the stomach infections can be accessed better if they are taken as a suppository. In the old days, the Romans often took medicine in this way. Especially if you have stomach upsets and so forth. The bullet things dissolve once inserted."

"Err," said Sammy. "Fat toffs do that when they are on a diet."

This time, Sister Ciara and Harry the convict looked confused. They both stared at one another puzzled and then back at the youngster.

"Why would fat people on a diet do such things?" asked Sister Ciara. She was intrigued.

"I don't know," replied the youngster. "I just heard others talking about it once."

"What others?" said Harry. "The toffs that do that sort of thing are a bit funny. It has nothing to do with diet."

Once again, Sister Ciara was confused by the language. "How are we on funny toffs that diet, all of a sudden?"

Harry looked at Sister Ciara and decided to let the nun in on a little secret. "Funny toffs that are bent, Sister."

Again she frowned. "Funny toffs that are bent?"

Harry nodded. "Yes, Sister you get a lot of funny toffs that like that sort of suppository thing. You hit the nail on the head when you said Romans. I think they invented most strange things."

"They are just on a diet," exclaimed Sammy. "They don't eat things. They do that suppository thing."

"No, it does not mean that at all, Sammy," replied the old convict.

"Yes, it does," replied the street urchin, with ill-deserved confidence.

"It does not, Sammy." For once Harry was adamant.

Sister Ciara was like a spectator at a tennis match. Watching the two males batting replies back and forth. It was an amusing spectacle but she was trying to fathom out what was meant. She could make out that Sammy innocently thought people on diets resorted to taking suppositories instead of food. While Harry was of another opinion about toffs, or well-to-do gentlemen doing suppository things for a different reason. Then it suddenly came to her that Harry was trying to tell the boy about illicit and perverted individuals doing diabolical sexual things.

"Oh my God, Harry," Sister Ciara cut in. She reached forward and put her hands over Sammy's ears. "Don't go telling the young man about things like that."

"But the lad thinks toffs doing a suppository are blokes on a diet. I'm trying to tell him they are a bit ginger beer, that's all." Harry held his hand up and waved it down like a comical view of an effeminate man.

"He does not need to know things like that, Harry," scolded the nun.

Sammy pulled Sister Ciara's hands away from his ears. "I already know what a ginger beer is. Someone who is as bent as a nine-bob note. I'm saying some toffs on diets do a suppository instead of dinner."

Sister Ciara was wondering if it was she who was learning an awful lot.

"And that will make a toff into a ginger beer," added old Harry. "That's why they walk along wiggling their hips like woman. Suppositories turn blokes into ginger beers. I've seen it when a weird toff walks down the street."

Sammy screwed his face up and cheekily replied. "Oh, stop worrying, Harry, it was just a blooming toff that was chewing a toffee."

Sister Ciara gasped and put her hands over her mouth. She was trying to withhold the laughter. "Oh, my God! Will you men be stopping this type of talk now? It is awful, so it is."

Harry started chuckling too. This time he was holding his stomach. Like Sister Ciara, he could not contain the glee. His laughter was compelling and he suddenly roared a high pitch squeal of joviality. It was immensely infectious merriment. Sammy began to laugh with him. Then Sister Ciara began to giggle. She did not want to, but the little urchin always seemed to have something 'off the cuff' to say.

"Shush!" she pleaded. "The Martians might hear us."

"I think Harry might have scared them off," Sammy chuckled.

"Oh my Lord, Sammy you can be awful sometimes," she laughed. The boy was an old man trapped in a youngster's body. "Where did you learn to say such things?"

"He's a street urchin. A little tasty geezer." Harry was still giggling. "It's what he does. He's got the gift of a sharp cake hole and he set me up for that punch line."

"Did you, Sammy," giggled Sister Ciara. "I must say that was awful good, so it was now. But never let the other nuns hear quips like that." She continued to chuckle.

Sammy looked at the two adults as they giggled away. He had struck a chord and was feeling pleased with himself. He had a great fondness for Sister Ciara and a sympathetic understanding for the convicted criminal, Harry. In a world of Hell, he had met two very special people. A nun armed to the teeth with a hunter's rifle and belts of high-powered bullets. And a convicted murderer with an army rifle and a punch-drunk brain. They were very fine people and at this particular moment in time he could not think of a better place to be and of any finer company to keep.

The beans began to sizzle in the pot. Sister Ciara took it from the fire grating and began to stir the mushy contents. They smelt wonderful. Harry had opened the tin of corn beef. An orange tin with white writing.

"What does that say on the tin, Sister Ciara?" asked the youngster.

"Corn Beef on the top and below the picture it says Libby, McNeill & Libby. The black writing says Chicago. Therefore, I think it is American corned beef. I'm going to cut them into slices for us." She smiled excitedly.

Three plates were laid before them. A supper of sliced corn beef and beans was happily presented.

"A feast fit for kings," added Harry with a big cherubic smile. They were all feeling jovial from the dark and comical banter. Now for a sumptuous repast.

Sister Ciara handed Sammy a plate of corn beef and beans. The youngster thanked the matriarchal nun. She nodded her acceptance and then offered Harry his plate.

"Thank you, Sister Ciara." He looked about him as they sat cross legged on the floor in front of the crackling office fire place. "Well this is cosy."

"I could just live here all the time," agreed Sammy.

Sister Ciara nodded her approval too. "I've stayed in worse places."

Together they ate their fine supper. When they had finished, Sister Ciara poured out black tea. "No milk or sugar. So, this will be an acquired taste."

There were no complaints from anyone. They had eaten. The black tea with no sugar was fine – they had acquired the taste long ago.

"Did you ever smoke, Harry?" Sister Ciara smiled at the convict. "I mean before you went to prison. You look like a man who would have smoked."

"I used to love a smoke, Sister Ciara. What about you. I have seen a nun smoking."

"I do, and so did many of the nuns. But that was one the first things I noticed, once the invasion and all its consequences set in. The soldiers shot looters. Yet still, the tobacconists and the newsagents were among the first places hit." Sister Ciara pondered the memory.

"The soldiers were clearing all the whisky and beer from shops. We used to watch them when we were in hiding," added Sammy. "The biggest thieves ever were the soldiers. They had to hide from the Martians when they were defeated and London fell, but they would find ways of scurrying out to the shops. I saw them shoot looters and then watched as they looted themselves. It was no longer a war against the Martians. It was a war against looters. I even heard them arguing with soldiers from other areas. Each group of soldiers had their own patch. They owned all the shops. They even shot kids who tried to find food."

Sister Ciara nodded. "I know. The survivors of the defeated army became a law unto itself. Everything broke down. Some soldiers even tried to steal from us, in our sewer shelter. But Sister Cathleen, God bless her, stood her ground with them. I and Sister Margaret stood beside the Prioress."

"What happened?" Sammy was excited and intrigued.

"Nothing, in the end."

"There was an old sergeant who tried to bellow. Sister Cathleen bellowed back. He then tried to reason and we all reasoned back. There was a horde of children behind us. They were a valuable weapon.

The soldiers walked away from our sewer sanctuary. Some of them fled the city completely. The horrid old sergeant never returned. I saw his dead body about a week later. He was lying amid some rubble. All the signs were there. He had been taken by a Martian fighting machine. His body was sucked dry of blood. There were puncture wounds either side of his neck. His death would have been an awful one. Then his body had been cast aside, smashed against walls and fallen on the debris. I had no sympathy for him. He was a man with the complete self-conviction of vanity. He was in charge of a party of looters and no doubt had shot other looters. There was no longer a British army in London. Just vagabonds in uniform."

"So, did they take all the tobacco and drink?" asked Harry.

"I think most of the soldiers did that. Some looters probably got away. We were looking for medicines and food. However, I found some tobacco in the desk while you were out gathering beans and corn beef," said Sister Ciara delightedly.

"You never did," Harry was thrilled.

"I did so, Harry."

The nun cheerfully pulled out a full pouch of tobacco and cigarette papers. She started to roll a cigarette with dexterous ease. It was a good solid roll. She offered it to Harry.

He smiled and took the roll-up. "Thank you, Sister Ciara."

She rolled another and gave it to the twelve-year-old boy. "I know you are no angel, Sammy. But these are very exceptional times."

Sammy smiled and accepted the roll-up. The street urchin smoked, when he could get hold of tobacco. It was easy enough before the Martians came. "Thanks, Sister Ciara," he said gratefully.

"Lord knows we might not be here tomorrow," said the old unconventional nun. She rolled another and put it between her lips. She took a burning ember from the grating and held it before Sammy. He drew and puffed on his cigarette. Harry copied and did the same and then Sister Ciara lit hers.

They sat back and contemplated the world and all its madness. The fire crackled and bathed the room with a homely glow. The lamps also threw out a welcome radiance too.

"Tomorrow morning our quest starts anew," Sister Ciara said as she blew out a steady line of smoke.

Sammy was making little rings. Obviously a seasoned smoker at twelve. It was not unusual. Most of the street urchins were. Harry drew nervously and then closed his eyes as he inhaled.

"I'd all but forgot what a rolled tab was like," he muttered with satisfaction.

"Yes," Sister Ciara agreed. "I and some of the other nuns were awful bad tempered at first. It surprises me how a person can become grumpy without a cigarette."

"It took some time to get used to not having them," said Sammy as he took another draw. "We tried searching in some of the houses when we were hiding in Poplar. But soldiers shot two of my mates in our gang."

"I'm sorry to learn of this, Sammy. I take it this was before one of our foraging parties found you."

Sammy smiled and nodded. "That's right, Sister. It was one of the reasons that our gang decided to go through the tunnel to the south side. The army patrols were shooting on sight. It was their territory back then. Most have moved on now."

"When this Martian business is all over, and it will be soon, there will be other troubles. Law and order will be brutally enforced to begin with. Then gradually things will settle. At least, I hope it all will."

"We are in Purgatory now. Our main worry is the orphanage and the hospital in the sewer. We must get that medicine back to them," Harry said.

Outside, it had started to rain. Raindrops began to splatter against the office window. Sister Ciara stood up, walked to the office door and opened it. She sniffed in the air then looked back at Harry and Sammy. The nun smiled and threw her spent cigarette out into the downpour. "It smells fresh," she said. "Perhaps the world is cleansing itself."

"Yeah," replied Sammy. He got up and threw his cigarette into the rain. "Washing away the stench of the Martians."

"Rain is rain," said Harry. He was unimpressed.

Sammy gripped Sister Ciara's arm. It was sudden, and the boy held up his other hand with his index finger raised. He was straining to hear something through the rain.

"There are no Martians here, Sammy," whispered Sister Ciara. "We would hear them."

Then there came the distant sound of a giant footfall. It was far off, but then there was the sound of another. A little louder. Sister Ciara watched the ripples of vibration over the water drenched yard. "Oh my God," she whispered.

"It's coming this way," said Harry. He got up and walked out into the rain. He stood in the yard looking about him. Sammy came out too.

The youngster looked at the small chimney pot on top of the office building. Smoke was coming out into the rain.

"It will notice the smoke," said Sammy. "We got to get away from here. Martians always examine heat. They know it means people are about."

Harry and Sammy were beginning to get anxious. Another distant footfall hit the ground. It was louder. A fighting machine was getting closer.

Sister Ciara came out of the office. She had retrieved her rifle and was awkwardly carrying Harry's weapon with the two bags of medicine. "Take your gun, Harry."

The old convict quickly complied, while Sammy grabbed the medicine bags and put them in the wet pushcart.

"Wheel it under the stable sheds," Sister Ciara pointed to the wall where a rough corrugated lean-to stood on wooden posts.

"Aren't we going to run?" asked Sammy nervously. Another footfall. Getting closer. Getting louder. He wheeled the pushcart under the lean-to.

"Have you doused the fire?" Harry was about to go back to the office and put the blaze out.

The ground shook again and the ripples shimmered over the forming puddles.

"No, Harry. We leave the fire burning. These Martians persist in leaving their machines. I don't know why but they do. Also, I know this beauty," she tapped the hunting rifle. "It will penetrate that green window part. The fire is our bait. And running from the fighting machine is more dangerous than confronting it. Especially as we have learnt to use certain advantages."

Another footfall as the ground shook a little more forcefully.

Sammy's face lit up. Fear subsided and excitement began to grow. "Are you going to bag another one, Sister?" He called from the lean-to.

Sister Ciara looked through the rain and over to the youngster. She winked at him and smiled reassuringly. "I'm certainly going to give it a try, young Sammy."

Another footfall with a stronger shimmer across the puddles.

"Shall we split up again?" asked Harry. This was becoming an attack pattern. They were developing into seasoned Martian killers.

Another crashing footfall ripping through the downpour of rain.

"We will," replied Sister Ciara. "Sammy, stay close to the pushcart. Harry, find yourself a nice hiding place with a clear shot at the office door. If one comes out of the machine, it will want to explore the source of the heat. The fire will attract its attention. Wait until it is sitting snuggly in sight. Your rifle will kill the beast when outside of its machine. You know that now. You already brought one down outside the hospital. You can drop another. Of that I'm sure.

A further footfall beyond the night's deluge. The unseen machine was to be changing course. It was turning. They could hear the creak of its alien alloy.

"As for me and my little beauty," again she tapped the rifle. "I want a clear shot at the green window. Most are the two-type fighting machines. One might stay inside while one comes out."

Another crash, so much louder.

"It is almost here," said Sammy. He quickly ran for his chosen spot and hid in the shadows.

Sister Ciara climbed a set of steps and onto a small landing that overlooked the yard. She had just made the recess of a dark dingy doorway when the fighting machine homed into view. A green oval light was shining through the downpour. The splaying tentacles were whipping around. One was holding the round pipe shaped apparatus that unleashed the devastating heat ray. That feeler was the main concern.

One of its titanic legs came over the wall and smashed down upon the cobbled yard. Several puddles exploded under the colossal footfall. The fighting machine was not the height of the two-Martian machines. Not like most of the tripods, which Sister Ciara realised at once. This was a one-Martian machine, and her gun sight was pointing up at the green convex orb at the front of the body trunk. It was the same small design as the one they had taken at Shooter's Hill earlier during the day, before starting their quest. The same design that she knew her bullets could penetrate.

The Martian mechanism suddenly stopped. One leg in the work yard with the other two outside in the deserted rain-sodden street. The capsule suddenly started to lower from its high point. The sound of squeaking hydraulics as the container finally lay cradled between the three knee joints of the contraption. It was still about two yards above the top of the high wall and gates. Even though the whole vehicle had dropped by about three yards.

"My God," whispered Sister Ciara. "Why do these things venture out of their machines? Especially when alone. It does not make sense. Why have they not learnt to fear us? They should have learnt by now."

The machine's mechanical appendages stretched and began to lower before the office door. The snake-like feelers went through the entrance on a controlled exploration mission. It would detect the fire inside, still crackling away. The tentacle holding the heat ray also lowered. The weapon device covered the doorway. For a moment, all three human onlookers froze, expecting a whirr of the Martian gun before discharging its heat ray into the small office building. It never came.

Instead, from the alien capsule came the usual click of a mechanism unlocking. Slowly, a side compartment door opened upwards. Beneath the body trunk was an array of small lighting. Shafts of dreary green ambience bathed the work yard. The puddles splashing away amid the cascading rain drops.

Harry watched from the dark shadow of his hiding place. He thought to himself. "Oh, come on you little beauty. Come to Harry and I'll give you a nice big shiny bullet to chew on."

All three waited expectantly, each breathing through their nostrils and exhaling via mouth. All with weapons ready. The times this strange thing occurred was beginning to become almost predictable. The same question came to each person lying in wait.

Why? When would these Martians learn? What strange stupidity made them make the same mistake every time they came upon a heat source? None of the human ambushers were complaining. In fact, all were comfortable with the routine and predictable Martian behaviour. It was becoming an almost guaranteed mode of kill. A trusted routine.

The towering machine stood motionless in the cascading rain. A dim light from the open door of the office cast a flickering light against the under carriage. In turn, the crisscross of the fighting machine's green spotlights shone down, showing the raindrop explosions of the plunging drops hitting the puddles. The whole work yard had become a theatre of small, focused lights. An arena waiting for an event. An audience waiting for an entertainer, in the shape of a vulgar, three-legged creature from Mars. The three humans watched with expectancy and wicked glee from their carefully chosen shadowed confines.

Again, Sammy watched as he relived the experience of the grey fleshy feelers with their three long fingers gripping the open door way. He knew one French word. Someone once told him what it meant. Now the twelve-year-old boy whispered it to himself amid the pouring rain.

"*Déjà vu.*"

Slowly, Sammy raised his revolver in readiness. His little piece of anti-Martian faith. Then came the expected sight of the hideous Martian. The one-Martian machine, and the sole occupant within. The alien occupier was going to emerge and venture into the yard. The vile thing stood upon its three thick legs at the capsule's opening. It had a rash of warts and carbuncled lumps. A quivering sweating epidermis of revolting imperfection. The bird-shaped beak with a line of ridges led up between the green oval eyeshades. Sammy thought the dark-green pools were staring straight at him. But only for a split second. There was a strange hissing from the creature as it turned to a side mechanism. Nimble arm feelers with equally adroit fingers worked a device upon the wall of the craft. Once again, Sammy remembered the strange lift that a previous Martian stood upon. There was a faint hum and the creature was suddenly aboard the contraption. In the cascading rain, the odious fat mound upon its three trunk legs was lowered towards the ground. It was like some strange trapeze artist in a demented off world circus.

It was fascinating to watch the disagreeable hulking form. The usual cylindrical container was on its back, with flex attached to the hand gun in one of its four feelers. It spryly turned and moved across the foundry yard in the pouring rain. The three legs operated in balanced cooperation, like a mammal. Yet there were no feet or hooves. There was just an end coiled tentacle. A foot, made from a twisted swirl. A slithering spring of flesh. It seemed to walk and skim at the same time. About its body mass were the four smaller tentacle arms, feelers with three fingers at each end. They were constantly moving about, the little fingers splaying and then closing. Then there were the even smaller dangling follicles. Repulsive clusters of worm-like hairs about the beak area of the creature. It stopped suddenly, looking towards the foundry entrance doors. Something had caught its attention. Perhaps a rat. It moved a little closer to investigate. Nothing, it stopped just short of the doors. The rain ran courses along the indentations and crevices of the grey hide, which looked as though it was riddled with disease.

Far off in the rain-drenched night came another alien call. "*Oolagh*," sang out across dead London

The Martian stood aloof and seemed to make a grunting sound. The creature looked up to its fighting machine and held aloft one of the smaller appendages. Within the three fingers was a small device. It clicked and immediately the empty fighting machine bellowed a reply.

"*Oolagh!*"

The sound was deafening, like an old river foghorn. It felt as though the yard would shake. It drowned out the sound of the cascading rain.

It muffled the sound of Sister Ciara's hunting rifle which had cracked out at the very moment the machine bellowed its reply.

Sammy caught the amazing spectacle in all its delightful wickedness. The powerful bullet entered the Martian's rear upper head area. It passed straight through. The alien face exploded outwards. A fountain of red, ruptured flesh splattered across the yard and over the doors. A fierce billow of brick dust rose where the high- powered bullet smashed into the wall column next to the bloody wooden gates. The Martian's three legs buckled. The creature's many feelers fell limply to its side as the monstrosity dropped into a seated position and then rolled forwards onto its pulverised excuse for a face.

"Job done! No king's horses and no king's men to put you back together again," Sammy whispered. But his malicious smile quickly faded to a look of concern. The distant fighting machine was answering the call. It let out a second distant rumble.

"*Oolagh!*"

Sister Ciara came down the gantry stairs. Harry emerged from the shadows too. The nun called to him. "We have to leave this place quickly. That other thing will be here very soon."

Sammy was wheeling the push cart out as Sister Ciara moved straight for the yard's large entrance doors. She slipped on the blood and gore but managed to stay upright. Harry, who was following was not so lucky. He slipped over and fell. As he did so, his army rifle clattered to the floor and went off. The bullet slamming into the wooden door close to Sister Ciara's foot.

She jumped and hissed. "For the love of God, Harry, let's get moving now. Pick yourself up quickly. We've no time to lose." She looked to Sammy who was pushing the cart past her and out into the dark street.

"I know another place," he called back at them as he made off into the night with the pouring rain swallowing him up.

"Wait for us, Sammy," called the old convict as he sped past the nun. He was covered in the blood and gore of the alien she had shot. Sister Ciara cursed and followed after them.

They were jogging through the darkness and the cascading rain. Around them were the deserted and wrecked buildings of the Martian apocalypse.

Harry ranted between breaths. "I don't know where all this bloody cloud came from, Sister. Before we went into the blooming office it did not seem too bad. Now it's raining."

"I think that one little perplexity is not worth our concern, Harry. The big three-legged bastard coming this way should take priority."

"Say what you mean, Sister," replied the convict. "Don't bother with polite chit-chat and all that usual stuff."

"It's over here," called Sammy as he veered off with the pushcart down a side street. Sister Ciara and Harry hurried after the youngster.

"We're going in the wrong direction. This is Woolwich. We want to go up Shooters Hill. We're moving along the river." Harry seemed concerned.

"Let's just be away from the approaching machine," replied Sister Ciara. "Just follow the boy."

The rain beat down with intensified ferocity. It was welcome, even though it was uncomfortable. Behind came another call of the fighting machine.

"I reckon that thing is getting close to the foundry by now." Harry called as the sudden distant sound of whirring sang out across the streets and abandoned buildings. "The heat-ray gun is winding up."

An explosion followed and they all stopped to look back. It was the foundry where they had been hiding. The area was bathed in flame and a larger two-creature Martian tripod was standing next to the smaller machine. Both titan contraptions were silhouetted against the glow of an expanding fire ball. Even through the cascading rain and the night. The scene from Hell was very clear.

"It does not wind up like a clockwork gun, Harry," said Sister Ciara.

"What is not clockwork," asked Harry. The fire ball bathed the streets in light, including the area where Sister Ciara and her companions were. The group quickly hid behind the corner of a building to watch the inferno.

"The Martian whirring sound that comes before it shoots its heat ray." Sister Ciara answered.

"Oh, I know, Sister. I just don't know how else to describe it." Harry was more concerned by something else that caught his attention. It was the huge leg of a dead fighting machine across the road from their place of concealment. The distant glow of the burning foundry bathed the lifeless contraption in sinister radiance. Harry looked up, high into the glowing rain-sodden night air. His sight stopped at the slumped body trunk. The capsule was suspended in the usual immobile stance, cradled down between three giant legs and looking more like a giant spider. "They always drop down to that hanging position when turned off or dead," he muttered.

Sister Ciara agreed. "Yes, that dormant stance does seem to be a trait with the tripods. Gladly, that one is well and truly dead. Look, there goes a rat crawling up the leg towards the carriage."

They all watched the rodent scurry up along the flexed vein like conduits that were along the elongated leg.

"Probably knows the green jelly thing that the tripods have as a window is gone. The crows and rooks would have sorted that out by now. The rat will see if the birds have left pickings of the Martian carcass inside."

"All Earth's creatures doing their bit." Sister Ciara said approvingly.

As they watched the rat reach the ruptured green porthole, they all recoiled in disgust. There was a multitude of rats scurrying all around the opening. Some going in, others coming out.

"Those things are getting fatter by the day," said Harry.

"There are plenty of feral cats about that will make sure the rats pay a price for their bounty of Martian flesh."

Sammy spoke. "We should keep moving, Sister."

"Lead on then, Sammy. We're right behind you, lad." The nun followed the boy, with Harry close on her heels. The firestorm at the foundry was behind them and they were all eager to put more distance between themselves and the fiery scene.

"Other fighting machines, if there are any, will be attracted to that fire," Sammy said as he pushed the cart through the rain.

"I'm sure we would rather that than the Martians trying to pursue us," Sister Ciara grinned. "Let us use the attraction to get further away."

"The fighting machine is still standing over the mess it's made," replied Harry, who had looked back nervously. The blaze was huge and the mobile machine was standing back as though surveying the carnage, expecting a human to crawl out. The other machine, that of the dead Martian, was slowly being consumed by the raging flames.

Harry made out the undercarriage of the bigger machine. The green glow of the lights displayed the side of the distant body trunk and the inferno also illuminated the Martian contraption. A side door opened upwards. The Martians were going through the same standard procedure.

Harry gasped. "There the buggers go again. They're coming out to explore the area. The two of them."

"At least it's not following." Sister Ciara slung her hunting rifle over her back and grabbed one of the cart handles to aid Sammy. Together, they pushed the stall onwards, with the armed old convict a few paces behind. The young street urchin certainly knew his way about, even at night in the dark and deserted streets of south east London.

They passed another dead tripod a few blocks on. The sterile monolith towered over the rooftops into the night. More food for the scavenging carrion and rats. The blight killing the Martians was apparent everywhere. For Sister Ciara's small group on their mission to acquire medicine, the blight was not working quickly enough. The disease was aggressive, but still some of the lingering Martians remained. The alien creatures still tried to function. They continued to feed – on human blood if they could get it.

At one point, the group stopped and took cover again. Another machine had made a distant call, like a deep brass instrument? It drifted through the rainy night from the west.

"*Aghloo!*"

"That one is a long way off," whispered Sister Ciara.

"Yeah, but they've got blooming long legs and they move quickly," Sammy replied. His cocky persona was returning.

"Gawd!" Harry muttered and then smiled. "You always got yourself a little off-the-cuff quip, ain't ya, boy."

Sister Ciara smiled at the banter. It all helped in the testing moments. "It's all part of the lad's service, Harry."

Sammy agreed. "Yeah, Sister. And at no extra cost."

The nun and the old convict chuckled. In the Hell on Earth – their vile Purgatory, they could lend warmth to each other with such trivial banter. It was a little extra firewood to feed the little bit of courage each had left. In a strange way, it worked.

Once again the surreal Catholic nun unslung her powerful hunting rifle. She went through the well-practised motion of taking a bullet from her gun belt and then pulling back and locking the bolt. Carefully, she placed the hefty bullet into the breach, then slammed the bolt forward. Her weapon was loaded and ready.

"Where to now, Sammy?" she asked, with a look of devilment on her face.

"I know a place just up here, Sister," replied Sammy.

"Lead on then. There's a good lad."

The rain continued to beat down relentlessly as the three entered the High Street of Plumstead. The distant destruction and radiating light almost drowned the noise of the cart's wheels over the cobbled road. Finally, they came to a stop before the Invicta football ground.

"We can go in here," Sammy said to Sister Ciara. The rain was running down his face and his sodden clothes.

She stood there holding her rifle. The rain was beating down on her face and spectacles. She squinted through the water-spattered lenses and looked up at the football ground's sign. "Royal Ordnance Factories. I once watched Woolwich Arsenal play football here. I came with Sister Maureen. Some years back. We can't get into the football ground, Sammy. The place would be locked. Very well locked."

"Yes, Sister, but my mates and I used to bunk in." The look of devilment was in his eyes.

"You bunked in?"

"Yeah, wait here a moment." He took a run at the wall. As he hit it with a leg out, he jumped and stepped against the wall at the same time. He just about managed to grab the top. The street urchin hauled himself up and dropped down the other side.

Sister Ciara looked to Harry and he shrugged. To the west, the sky was still ablaze with the fire from the destroyed foundry yard. The rain continued to beat down relentlessly. Shelter was hard to find. In the distance, the functioning tripod was still silhouetted against the roaring blaze. The flames had reached the abandoned smaller contrivance.

"Well, look at that, Harry, we shot the Martian and now its vehicle is succumbing to the flames of the foundry's destruction."

"Perhaps the Martians think we are in the buildings of the work yard," muttered Harry.

"Maybe," answered Sister Ciara. "Expecting us to come running out. I would suppose that the two Martians from the other machine are patrolling the perimeter looking for us."

Sammy emerged from a red wooden side door. "In here," he called, then jumped. An advertising boarding had fallen from the door. It showed a picture of a bearded sailor inside a naval life buoy with the words *Player's Navy Cut* around the ring. The word *Cigarettes* was fashioned outside of it, against a background of land and sea.

Sister Ciara trudged forward, her gun at the ready. She was soaking wet as she passed through the door. Harry followed, taking the duffel bags containing the medicines off the push cart.

"We'll have to leave the flower stall outside. It won't fit through the door," Harry said. "I'll chance leaving the tarpaulin. I doubt anyone will steal it."

"You should hide the pushcart too," advised Sammy. "In a doorway or something."

Sister Ciara frowned. "Are you sure, Sammy?"

"Yes, Sister. The Martians always seem to notice odd little things. When our gang used to hide from them, the Martian machine's feeler things always noticed stuff we left behind. Anything out of place. Even among the debris and wrecked things. They seemed to know what was new. A Martian in its tripod would notice a cart left by this door."

The nun looked to Harry. "Can you move the cart away into a bush or something? Somewhere hidden from observation at height. We need the cart covered or under something."

"Yes, Sister," replied the convict. Sammy and the nun waited in silence until the old man returned. The rain continued to pour. Harry closed the door upon returning and entering the football stadium.

"They'll notice if this door is open too," he advised.

"They would do, Harry," Sammy answered.

Sister Ciara shook her head in disbelief. "I can't understand how these Martian creatures can be so astute at spotting an abnormality like discarded debris amid debris then do something stupid like leave their machines and search for us with inadequate protection."

"We were like frightened sheep at first, Sister," replied Sammy. "I reckon Martians took that to their Bible. They don't understand that we can learn how to fight them back."

"You might have a point there, Sammy. They are full of unpredictable actions. Now there are not so many of them, they seem easier to trap and kill. They are devoid of caution and are running out of time to learn."

"Perhaps that is their weakness, Sister," suggested Harry.

The nun nodded her head in agreement. "Yes, Harry. It could be."

They walked along the perimeter of the football ground. They could only see the overgrown grass at the edge of the pitch. Even in the rain, the fire from the foundry was illuminating the night sky enough to make out the sight. The grass had grown long and wild like a field of crops.

"I reckon the pitch is almost like a wheat field." Harry raised his voice slightly to be heard through the cascading rain.

"There are signs of rotting remains too." Sister Ciara called amid the downpour.

"Rotting remains?" Sammy seemed confused.

Sister Ciara nodded. "The Martian red weed. It will soon be broken down by Earth's healthy germs. Eaten and fed as compost to the unkempt long grass of this football pitch."

"How do you know these things, Sister?" Harry asked.

"Yeah, do nuns have to learn about rotting things? Is it because nuns and the church bury dead people?"

Sister Ciara shook her head. She was amused. "No, Sammy, we don't learn because of burying people. Individual nuns learn certain things. I've just worked in horticultural areas at various nunneries. Horticultural means farming and growing of plants. I know that all living things break down and rot. They are devoured by tiny germs and these are all in the soil. Other plants eat this with water when it rains. I'm not an expert, but I have worked among people who could be considered well-informed on such matters."

"So, our plants are eating the Martian plants?" Sammy looked very hopeful.

Sister Ciara smiled. "Yes, young man. In a manner of speaking."

Sammy clenched his fist, and through gritted teeth he excitedly punched the air with gratification. "Yes! That is champion."

"We need to find some shelter," said Harry.

It was dark, cold and the rain was still intense. They stuck to the perimeter and arrived before the player's tunnel area, a hallway beneath the spectators' seating.

Sammy went in to the darkness first. He held one of the duffel bags full of medicines. Sister Ciara held the other. The boy spoke as they tested the changing-room doors. "Everywhere is dark and spooky."

"No more so than out here, young Sammy. You English have a gift for understatement," sighed Sister Ciara.

Harry, oblivious to the nun's quip, said. "These doors open but there is just a stone floor and changing benches. Not really a place to sit down in, Sister. There's not much going on inside this room."

"That has a certain irony too Harry." Sister Ciara smiled bitterly. "Not even a candle light on."

The brutish man grinned back and nodded his head. Then he frowned with confusion. "I don't think anyone would leave a candle light on, Sister. I certainly wouldn't."

Sammy could not resist grinning back at the nun. "Is that understatement too, Sister?"

She looked down at the street urchin. Her brown eyes glared through her thick-rimmed spectacles and her nostrils flared. The old nun's jaw was fixed grim. Yet somewhere within that stern look, Sammy detected the supressed humour. It might as well have been a face made of jelly. Made in a severe mould, but transparent nonetheless.

He continued to grin back at her. In the end, Sister Ciara raised a humorous eye-brow and let the boy have his moment.

Then they came upon the director's office, which was locked. Sister Ciara sighed.

"That is one place that would have been more comfortable."

"That's a shame," replied Harry. "I bet the toff who runs this place has a nice set of comfy chairs."

"Is there any way we can get it open?" Sister Ciara asked.

Harry's big boot hit the door by the lock. The latch caved in and broke open instantly. He looked to the nun and the young street urchin with a satisfied smile. "I'm going back to the changing rooms. I noticed a line of sinks. An ablutions area. I want to see if I can clean this Martian gore off of me. Blast slipping at the foundry gates. Even the rain hasn't washed it off."

"That is a good idea, Harry." Sister Ciara smiled at the big brutish man. "Sammy and I can wait in here."

"You will not be able to use a lamp, Harry." added Sammy. "The Martians might see the glow through the changing-room glass."

"There is just about enough light from the foundry fire. The glow was coming through the changing-room window. Enough for me to see. I can manage without a lamp." Harry left and returned to the dark changing room.

Sister Ciara watched the old convict go to attend to his need. Then she looked down at Sammy and smiled.

"Well, young man. In we go."

"Have you got anymore roll ups, Sister?" Young Sammy was becoming more relaxed with the rebel nun. They entered the tidy little office.

"I have, but don't go getting relaxed with such requests in front of the Prioress or the other nuns.

They will throw a biblical hissy fit with me. I'm not on their special nuns list, you know. I'm more of your doghouse nuns list."

Sammy grinned as he watched Sister Ciara take out the tobacco pouch. She started to roll a well-crafted cigarette. Upon completion, the nun handed it to Sammy and lit a match, shielding the naked flame with her cupped hands. The boy leaned forward and drew against the flame.

"God, I think I'm a female Fagin and you are another Artful Dodger. We'll share that one, Sammy. I want to preserve the tobacco as best I can."

"Right ho, Sister." He blew out a stream of smoke and handed the cigarette to her. "When did you come here to watch a football match then?"

"It was a few years back now." Sister Ciara drew on the cigarette and blew out a steady stream of smoke. "Sister Maureen is the Scottish nun. You've probably seen her working in the sewer hospital."

"Probably," replied Sammy. "But I can't tell the difference between Irish and Scottish accents. They all sound the same to me. I thought most nuns were from Ireland."

Sister Ciara laughed at Sammy's innocence. "So, you cannot tell the difference of an Irish accent to that of a Scottish? And you think most nuns are Irish? Why is that?" Amused, she handed the cigarette back to the boy.

"Well," he said before taking a drag and handing the cigarette back. He blew out a steady stream of smoke. "I thought nuns were invented in Ireland because nuns are Roman Catholics. That's why nuns come here. To make us all Catholics."

Sister Ciara laughed. "Nuns were not invented in Ireland, Sammy. There are all sorts of nuns and they are not all Catholic nuns either." She drew on the cigarette and gave it back to the, *sometimes*, naive boy.

"Oh," said Sammy. "So, do Catholic nuns come from Scotland?"

"No, from Rome in Italy. That is where the Pope lives."

"I've heard of the Pope and Rome." He was excited at knowing that part. He took another draw on the cigarette and gave it back to Sister Ciara. "He makes saints. He makes lots of saints. How does he decide who to make saints?"

"I suppose pious and devoted people make requests to the Pope." She put out the butt in an ashtray upon the director's dusty desk.

"So, why did you and the Scottish nun come here – to a football match?"

"It was when the Woolwich Arsenal played here. Sister Maureen was a huge fan of Hibernians. This football team's local rivals are Hearts of Midlothian. She wanted to watch this Scottish club when they came south to play Woolwich Arsenal. We had to attend in our civilian clothes because Sister Maureen said that Hearts were a Protestant club, as opposed to Hibernian being more Catholic. It would not have been appropriate to wear a nun's habit at such a game. I think she wanted to capture the old spirit of when she watched games back in Edinburgh. She said she watched Hibernian v Hearts of Midlothian often when she lived in Scotland. Then one of these teams came south all the way to London to play the Woolwich Arsenal. I think she was trying to chase a nostalgic moment. Here at this ground. It was a few years back now."

"Who won?" asked Sammy.

"Hearts won the game, five goals to Arsenal's one. Midlothian were the Scottish national champions, I think. They had just won a big cup up in Scotland. At least, that was what Sister Maureen told me."

"A different team play here now. Woolwich Arsenal moved to another ground." Sammy looked up at a small rectangular window. The rain was still running down it. The place was eerie and hollow. No echo or feel of the football players or the owners of the club. He looked around the wall and saw a picture of the Prince of Wales and Princess Alexandria in an open carriage with horses. The procession appeared to be going through Blackwall Tunnel.

"It was the opening ceremony," said Sister Ciara looking at the same photo. "A year ago, I think."

"I was waiting at the other end," said Sammy. He looked around at a small trophy cabinet. "Not much to boast about in here."

"Perhaps they took all of the cups when leaving the place."

"I don't think they won anything. Royal Ordnance Factories, I mean. Woolwich Arsenal went professional. That is why they went to another ground. They started to attract bigger crowds."

"I heard this place put the rent money up and the Woolwich Arsenal went elsewhere."

"Might have been that too," added Sammy. "Do they have to pay rent money then?"

"Of course they do. A ground like this would not come cheap."

The office door opened and Harry came in with a big cherubic smile on his face. His prison uniform was wet, where he had been crudely scrubbing it. The blood stains were still apparent, but the gore was removed. The old convict seemed pleased with his efforts. He was also holding a huge bundle of white industrial towels.

"These are the Royal Ordnance Factories' towels. A bit plush for the workers. I thought you might make use of them."

"That is very thoughtful, Harry," said Sister Ciara. "I'll try and dry down in the other changing room."

"There is no light, Sister. "Except for a small glow from the foundry fire."

"That'll have to do, Harry." Sister Ciara turned and went to the door. "Are the water taps working?"

"Yes, Sister," replied the convict. He looked to Sammy and threw a bundle of towels at the youngster. "Try and dry yourself down a bit, lad. Even a little damp is better than being drenched through."

Sammy smiled and took off his worn and shredded jacket. He then began to wipe his hair dry.

CHAPTER 9

THE LAST PART OF THE QUEST

They had fallen asleep. Not a deep sleep, for it was troubled. This was the nature of the times. Even in the sewer sanctuary, sleep was often broken and sporadic. This slumber had the usual troubled patches in the dark confines of the football ground's office. The glow of the foundry fire was still apparent in the night air. All saw it through the little window in moments of wakefulness. The good news was that the rain had stopped much to everyone's delight. A mental note before rolling over and trying for more sleep. When awake, ears strained for the tell-tale crash of a Martian machine. There were none – at least, no one heard anything.

It was well past three in the morning when Sister Ciara woke. Sammy's hand was gently pressing upon her mouth. It was to stop her from calling out. The

index finger of the other hand was over his lips –
a gesture to remain silent. She looked puzzled but
Sammy pointed to the closed office door. The lock
had been broken earlier. They had jammed the back
of a chair against the door handle before trying to
sleep. That very door handle was now gently turning. The resistance of the tilting chair was in play.
Someone or something was trying to quietly open
the door. Access was denied. The door was firmly
jammed shut. The busted fragments of the forced
door would surely have been noticeable to a human.
Would a Martian assume a forced entry? Could they
deduce such a thing in a city full of wrecked and broken things? Had Martian exploration groups been
inside the corridors before? It was feasible. Therefore,
such a change to the door would be noticed.

Sister Ciara sat up. Her heart was thumping
wildly. She tried to contain the anxiety inside. A blos-
soming dread and overwhelming fear. Yet somehow
she fought that inner battle. Her face was drained,
but the nun began to think pragmatically. Who or
whatever it was must know or suspect something.
How had the Martians deduced they were here?
What had lured them? Why were they exploring the
football ground?

She gripped Sammy's hand and pointed to
Harry who was sleeping. Silently she mimed "Wake
him."

Sammy nodded his head and stealthily moved towards Harry. He woke the old convict the same way that he had woken the nun. Harry woke and looked to the door handle where Sammy was pointing. He mimed, "They are in the hallway."

Harry nodded his head and stood up quietly. He had his rifle ready, as did Sister Ciara. He then looked and pointed to the old rectangular window high against the office wall. The workplace was slightly below ground and the elevated window was on ground level outside.

Sister Ciara gently lifted the owner's chair by the desk. Slowly and cautiously, she made towards the wall where the window was. Placing it gingerly below the window frame, she beckoned Sammy to come over with the duffel bags containing the medicine. The boy complied.

Again she mimed. "Test the window latch."

Sammy nodded. He handed the medical bags to Sister Ciara and stood on the chair. Gently, he eased the latch up and was able to push the window open. Thankfully, it did not squeak. Sister Ciara stood beside him. She gestured for the boy to get through the window. Nervously, the youngster complied. He was nimble and quickly through. The medicine bags followed.

The night air had a chill breeze after the recent rain, but it refreshed his anxious senses as did the gravel. The sensation smacked him with practical resolve. His first instinct was to check the immediate surroundings. He could see through the night's gloom and the gentle bathing light from the far-off foundry that continued to burn. There was nothing except the long grass of the football pitch and the upper parts of the old goalposts. They usually took them down in the summer months. The Invicta ground had left theirs out. Why dwell on such things in a time of crisis? He shook his head. Back to the immediate task. He beckoned Sister Ciara to follow. She placed her hunting rifle through the window onto the wet gravel. Harry was lifting her from inside while Sammy helped pull her unceremoniously out into the night air. So far so good.

Sister Ciara took a deep breath and surveyed her surroundings too. Meanwhile, Harry put his army rifle out onto the gravel. He was struggling while Sammy was pulling him through the window with every ounce of strength he possessed.

The convict rolled out over the wet shingle and picked up his Lee-Enfield rifle. The unkempt man took a deep breath and smiled at Sammy. He nodded his head approvingly, and ruffled the lad's hair. An indication of gratitude.

Again, Sister Ciara mimed the words. "Let's go." She had slung her rifle and was holding the medicine bags.

Together, they made their way around the perimeter of the ground. Past the goal post of the pitch's north bank stand. Harry stopped them abruptly. He indicated for all to go over the wall into the spectator's terrace. Sister Ciara and Sammy complied. Hidden behind the wall, Harry pulled an alarmed face and was pointing back towards the office area from where they had fled. Carefully, Sister Ciara and Sammy raised their heads to see what had caused the old convict to be alarmed.

Above the spectators' seating area at the changing rooms from where they had fled was the reason for Harry's alarm. Beyond the ground's walls stood the titanic form of a Martian tripod. It was the usual colossus of a contrivance and in the normal stance of immobility. The trunk was lowered between the three legs. Cradled many yards closer to the ground. The side panel was open and no doubt two Martians had emerged to explore the ground.

"It's the machine that blew up the foundry. How did they know where to search for us?" whispered Sammy.

"We hid the push cart in the doorway. It would be terrible bad luck for them to spot that," added Harry.

"Would they have noticed the cigarette advert that fell from the door?" asked Sister Ciara. "That is roughly where the tripod has stopped."

"Oh, blooming hell. If the Martians noticed it and stopped to investigate, they would come down from the machine. They would have then noticed the pushcart in the overhang of the bushes. It was hidden close to the door where the advert was. They always notice weird things like that." Sammy frowned. What horrendous bad luck.

Harry alerted them to danger. "Out there in the long grass," he whispered.

Sammy and Sister Ciara looked through the gloom. The long grass was moving. Something was progressing through the pitch's overgrown turf towards the stand where they were concealed. The crunch of gravel made them look back along the perimeter of the ground. Along the very path they had come, a second movement. In the gloom the group made out the physique of the three-legged alien walking and slithering over the gravel. The bulbous body with its backpack and conduits stopped as the second Martian appeared out of the long grass. It had been moving through the pitch towards the stand. The two Martians seemed to be communicating. For a moment they stood still.

"I'll take the right hand one. You go for the left, Harry." Sister Ciara whispered as she raised her rifle gently onto the stand wall.

"Will do, Sister," Harry answered in hushed tones.

"Let them get closer," added Sister Ciara. "We can't afford to miss. If one gets back to the machine, we will be in a very difficult situation."

Sammy had his revolver ready in case either missed. He looked on as tension gripped all. Harry was aiming at his target and Sister Ciara had her Martian prey in the gun sight of the hunting rifle.

The two Martians finished their hushed gurgling communication. Then they turned and began to walk stealthily along the gravel. Sammy was mesmerised by the thick leg tentacles, coiled at the bottom into a crude form of foot. The three legs were incredibly nimble. They functioned well. The creatures moved as though wary of something observing them. Yet still they moved exposed to the guns, almost as if they did not know how to take the precaution of evasive action. The creatures were now fighting outside of their machines. They were much more vulnerable and less adapt, especially when human beings got in close.

Harry whispered excitedly as the Martians came forward. "Come on, you silly bastards. Up close and dirty is the way we like it."

"Upon my order, Harry." Sister Ciara said in hushed tone. "Three, two, one – fire!"

The elephant gun and the Lee-Enfield rifle roared together. Sister Ciara's target opened its beaked mouth as the bullet hole appeared just above and between the dark-green eye shades. A fountain of blood and gore erupting behind the vile Martian as the high-powered projectile ripped its way out of the alien flesh. The ugly bulk covered in an insipid epidermis fell neatly into the usual sitting position as all three legs went limp and buckled inwards. The lifeless monstrosity rolled backwards.

Harry's Martian target was to the left side. A fountain of blooded gore swirling as the creature twisted. Its three legs were entwined like a crude plait of hair. Its hideous screams tore out in the night. Sammy jumped over the wall with his hand gun ready.

Sister Ciara was putting another powerful bullet into her rifle. Harry was pulling the bolt back on his army rifle.

"Careful, Sammy," called Sister Ciara.

The boy walked quickly along the gravel with a sense of purpose. He moved towards the squealing alien. He could see it had dropped its small heat gun. It was attached to the flex and the injured Martian was making no attempt to pull the weapon closer by the attachment. Instead the screaming creature held up one of its thin arm feelers. It was pointing to the far-off fighting machine beyond the stadium walls. Sammy realised that it was the device that could send a message to the machine. The Martian in the foundry had done the same before being shot. It could make the machine's strange speaker call out. Quickly, Sammy raised his gun as he heard the alien device click. The revolver fired three rapid shots into the bulk form of the already injured Martian. The fighting machine suddenly let out a deep bellowing call.

"*Arlugh!*"

The hideous roar rang out in the night.

Sammy put two more shots into the already dead Martian. The damage was done. The device had been triggered. The call had gone out.

"Quick, Sammy," called the old convict. "We got to be away from this place."

"What about the pushcart and the tarpaulin you wanted? We can go back and get it now."

"We'll come back for it another time," said Sister Ciara. "We have the much-needed medicine in the bags. We must move now. As quick as possible."

From the west came the responding Martian call. A distant bellow of a fighting machine, somewhere in the inner city.

"Let's not dwell on this now. We need to be away from here," said Sister Ciara. Pragmatism was setting in. She picked up the two valuable bags of medicine and made for the further side of the ground. All were very concerned. They needed to be away from the stadium. No doubt another Martian machine was on its way. The distant call rang out again, this time a little louder. A sign that another Martian contraption was answering the call of its dead comrades.

"Let's be gone while they search this area," whispered Harry.

By the corner of the ground, where the north bank joined the eastern enclosure, they found an emergency door. It was easily unlocked and they were out of the ground and into the deserted streets once again.

"Close the door as best as we can," said Sister Ciara.

Harry complied. Then turned to follow the nun and the youngster. Hastily they made their way up a residential road towards the direction of Shooter's Hill, at the top of which would be the welcome sight of a particular manhole cover. The point of salvation would still take some time to reach, but it would lead to a system of sewer tunnels, their sanctuary. But the valiant group had a long trial ahead of them. It was still dark, and the journey remained as demanding as ever. The new Martian crew of an approaching tripod would be searching for them very soon. Humans were scarce now and the ailing creatures were desperate to feed on blood. Human blood was a dwindling commodity, and reinforcements from Mars had ceased. The stranded abominations were battling for survival. Their plight had never been more hopeless, but it would not stop them trying to feed. The Martians would not become extinct quietly.

"I can't believe we've lost all that clean tarpaulin," hissed Harry, disappointed.

"It is not lost, Harry. As I've already said, we'll send a foraging party to collect it. We know where it is. I doubt anyone else will want or find it," said Sister Ciara reassuringly.

"Sister Ciara is right, Harry. We can just wheel the barrow back in a few days," added Sammy. "We'll let the dust settle then come back."

The brave band jogged on through the dark and deserted streets. Sister Ciara and Sammy each carried a duffel bag upon their back. The medical supplies had to be delivered.

Sammy began to reload his revolver while on the move. Sister Ciara was with her rifle. She had reloaded back at the stadium. Harry had done the same with his rifle. Soon all guns were in readiness when Sammy had completed his loading routine.

"Not just for the Martian threat, but also the dog packs," added the boy holding the revolver up.

Sister Ciara nodded. "Fortunately, the canine risk has lessened. Dogs tend to stay away from us old masters."

"All foraging groups have been told to remain vigilant of dog presence," said Harry.

"We shall, Harry," Sister Ciara smiled as the group jogged along the street.

Burnt and blackened skeletons lay here and there, human and horse, victims of past heat-ray attacks. Deserted carts, omnibuses and carriages were everywhere. The whole world had just come to a grinding halt. The deserted and sterile things of man's former world were garnished with a more sinister abandonment. The giant fighting machines from Mars had started to grind to a halt as well. Here and there, the colossal devices just stopped working and stood still. The odd one had fallen over, but most just stood immobile. Food for the many scavengers – the unkindness of rooks and many a murder of crows, the abundance of rats who seemed to be multiplying. Groups of feral cats were hunting and feeding on the rats, who were paying the price of earning an honest living. Then there were the feral dog packs. They had often been victims of the Martians, too. Yet when the aliens ventured out of their machines, the dogs seemed to have an instinctive blood lust for the extra-terrestrial flesh. It was as though all forms of Earth life were alert to the aliens from Mars. It appeared to be an instinct that most mammals, birds and even germs were predetermined to attack. All except humans. They had to learn. But learn they did. Weaknesses were being found and weaknesses were exploited. On Earth, the Martians were now doomed. They still killed but could not function much longer. It was all a matter of time. It was no longer a matter of *if* the Martians perished, but *when*.

Yet in the time the Martians had left, people could still die. People in the sewer sanctuary would still die, but perhaps the foraging groups could lessen the numbers. Sister Ciara and her unconventional team were determined to contribute to saving as many lives as possible. They were feeling satisfied with their foraging. The last steady run through the dead streets was all that was needed.

"We've certainly bagged ourselves a few Martians on this jaunt," added Harry. "I don't think any foraging group has claimed so many in one outing."

"Well, let's not count our chickens just yet, Harry. We've got to get back first."

"We have got eight of them so far," said Sammy. "That has got to mean something. I don't know anyone who has managed that many."

"That is between three of us, a pack of rats and a pack of dogs," Sister Ciara replied with a grin on her old face. "We can't be telling exaggerated stories."

"I shot the one the rats were eating," Sammy boasted. "And I got the one the dogs finished later. Plus the other back at the stadium. The one Harry injured. They all count."

"The boy is right, Sister." Harry was in agreement. "It's your holy work. We have been encouraged by your Godly presence. You have been sent by God."

As they continued to move along the dark streets, Sister Ciara tried to reply diplomatically. She did not want to hurt the feelings of the simple man and boy with her. "We must not get too carried away about the Godly aspect of my slaying of Martians. You lads have performed admirably. I'm very impressed by what you have managed to do."

Sammy did not want the nun to deny her divine importance to them. "Harry is right, Sister Ciara. We did it because of you. It was a Godly thing. God is helping us because you are here. It's all the prayers you have done in your life."

"This is my Purgatory, Sister Ciara," Harry was of the same opinion as the boy. "You have redeemed me into Purgatory. I have been given a chance of Heaven because of you."

Sister Ciara regarded both the simple men – she could not think of two better companions. Two veterans of trials and tribulations before the coming of the Martians. "I'm absolutely positive that God will let both of you worthy men into the kingdom of Heaven. God bless you both." She made the sign of the cross over her bullet belts, gripping the hunting rifle in the other hand.

CHAPTER 10

BACK TO THE BEGINNING

They pressed on through the scattered, rotting death and carnage, looking back now and then. The now distant foundry was still burning in the night, a distant glow miles back. They were moving along the main road and up the hill.

"Another fighting machine by the Invicta stadium. Look!" said Sammy pointing over the rooftops towards the football ground. Another fighting machine was standing next to the vacant one.

"No doubt they are discovering that two more of their comrades are dead." Sister Ciara sounded concerned.

"Soon the new Martians will begin to search for us." Harry called back to the nun. She had briefly stopped to take in the new situation.

"They'll get out and take a look around," added Sammy. "That will waste a bit of time."

"They can take as long as they like," replied Sister Ciara as she caught up. "I would not want them putting themselves out for us."

For once the humour was not lost on Harry. "No, best not put themselves out. I'm sure we can put up with being overlooked."

"They'll search about the changing rooms for a while," added Sammy hopefully.

Sister Ciara thought back to the conversation she had had with the Prioress before getting permission to go on this venture. "The Martians are woefully incautious. They'll never learn. The ghastly creatures seem very quick on some things, but less astute on more obvious matters."

"That's why we get to bag so many of them now." Sammy was feeling more positive.

"Yes, but I think we have been riding our luck a bit. I don't fancy another encounter with the Martians. I think we have had our fair share of conflict over the past day."

The nun spoke for all. They did not want to do anything that might encourage the new fighting machine to continue its search up Shooter's Hill, the place they were making for. Another colossal structure on the hunt would be more of a problem than any of the adventurers wanted. It was imperative they keep moving on.

Finally, they emerged from a side street onto another main road. The night air was still chilly, but it helped them stay alert. It was the very main road they had come down during the day as they approached the Blackwall Tunnel. The collapsed fighting machine they had passed earlier was once again before them. Its form was illuminated by the bleak light of the distant foundry fire. Cautiously they approached the smashed configuration and noted that the green porthole viewer facing the dark sky was all but gone. The carrion or rats had no doubt eaten it away.

A fat cat startled them. It emerged from the machine's porthole. Inside its mouth was the limp body of a rat.

"Well, each to their own," whispered Sister Ciara.

They ducked beneath the vast elongated legs and continued up the main road, which led to the top of Shooter's Hill.

"Let's be keeping this pace up, boys," panted Sister Ciara. "The manhole cover is at the top, and our sewer network will be nearby."

"That one works for me," replied Sammy.

At that moment, the horned bellow of the fighting machine erupted over the derelict rooftops.

"It's the machine by the Invicta football stadium. The Martians must have finished or abandoned their search." Sister Ciara was once again concerned.

They could hear the colossal contraption start to move. Sammy caught a glimpse between two buildings. The view was downwards and over more rooftops. All was still bathed in the hue of the distant burning foundry.

"It's coming this way," said the boy.

"Quick," called Harry as he made for the front garden of a derelict well-to-do house. "Let's hide in here."

Sister Ciara and Sammy reluctantly followed. The front door was open. Many of the residential houses had their street doors kicked in. They entered the front room. The windows were smashed and the night breeze was coming through.

"We may have been better off chancing the last little part of the journey, Harry," said Sister Ciara. "We are but a short distance from the top."

Sammy was observing and listening. The first thunderous footsteps began to crash. "It's coming this way," he said fearfully.

"It will spot us in the open, Sister." Harry was concerned too.

Sister Ciara frowned as the thumping steps grew louder. "My God, you're right, Harry."

"Stand away from the window," advised Sammy.

"Shall we go out the back way?" Sister Ciara asked.

Harry looked to Sammy. So did the nun. The two adults were wanting advice from the street urchin.

"Not yet," he advised. "Let it look about. It will be scanning the entire area. We stand more chance under cover. That thing is looking for us. The Martians are finding blood hard to come by."

"You mean they are starving?" Sister Ciara asked.

"I think so, Sister. Things have changed over the weeks."

"They're desperate, Sister." Harry added.

Suddenly, the machine's long leg stepped over a row of terraced houses and slammed down upon the cobbled road further down the hill. The body structure came into view against the night sky above the rooftops. The entire mechanism turned to look up the main road. The green porthole was glowing around the silhouette of something looking out. The immense device took a few giant strides up the hill and stopped outside the very dwelling where the fugitives were hiding. Everyone ducked for cover. There was an abundance of furniture for concealment. Outside came the mechanical humming sound. The internal working of the contrivance seemed laboured louder than usual.

Sammy gasped, "It can't know we are in here."

Sister Ciara had a look of abject terror. "Surely not."

Suddenly, the huge legs moved away from their view. The giant steps moved onwards up the hill, away from their hiding place. The tension immediately subsided, replaced by a welcome sense of ease.

"Oh, thank Christ for that," muttered Sammy.

They all sighed with relief as Sister Ciara admitted. "I think my notion of continuing to run up the hill would have proved fatal." She nodded at Harry with a look of gratitude. "Well called, Harry."

"Thank you, Sister," replied the gruff man. "Pleased to have done something of good."

"What should we do now?" Sister Ciara asked. She clutched her prized hunting rifle.

"There are backyards along the houses." Sammy said. "We could follow the machine up the hill while concealing ourselves in the alleyways behind the yards."

"They do not go right the way up to the top, do they?" Sister Ciara looked with renewed hope.

"They end at side streets. We'll have to run across them and into the next block's rear walkways. It goes most of the way up." Sammy was using his knowledge to good effect.

"Come on, then. Let's do as the lad suggests," said Harry.

Sister Ciara walked to the back door and went out into the back yard. She could hear the tripod beyond as it moved up hill. Sammy and Harry came out to stand with her.

"Do we have everything?" Sister Ciara asked.

Sammy turned slightly to display the duffel bag on his back with its valuable contents of medicine. The nun smiled and turned to show her duffel bag upon her back.

"Let's get to it then, Sister," said Harry. He walked to the rear yard wall where there was a wooden door. He undid the latch and it opened easily. Quickly, the group moved out into the dark walkway that went along the back of all the rear gardens.

"Move slowly," advised Sister Ciara. "We have no need to rush while that great thing is ahead of us." There were wild shrubs and stinging nettles that had grown out of control. But each managed to get by the untidy mess that the back walkways had become. At one point, they passed the rotting corpse of a dead old lady. She was a mere skeleton in clothing. No doubt the rats and dogs had been at her. It was not tainted with black resin. Therefore, she had been a food source for the feral animals, which seemed to be multiplying everywhere.

"Perhaps the Martians will keep going and bugger off into Kent," said Sammy, full of hope.

"Well, Kent is quite nice this time of year." Sister Ciara was feeling a little more relaxed.

"Not if the red weed is everywhere." Sammy smiled.

"The red weed is long dead," added Harry.

They got to the end of the alleyway and, confirming Sammy's advice, they came out on a side road. Quickly, they crossed and were back in another dark, claustrophobic alleyway, making their way behind more rear yards of residential property, more wet nettles and overgrown shrubs. Ahead of them, the machine was moving at a quicker pace. Its machine's footfall was growing fainter with each huge stride.

"It's putting a lot of distance between us and it," Sammy said delightedly.

"Won't get any complaints from me," Harry answered.

At the end of the next alleyway they stopped to reconsider the situation of their final run. This was the last part of the journey towards the inviting manhole cover and the inviting stench of their disease-ridden sewer sanctuary.

"Should we chance the main road?" asked Sister Ciara. "The machine has gone beyond the point of our goal. It might be quicker to take the main road now."

"I think we might chance it," agreed Sammy.

They looked to the old convict for his opinion. The gruff man nodded his head in compliance. "I reckon it would be all right to go back onto the main road."

The agreement was made. All three quickly emerged from the side street onto Shooter's Hill. They made their way upwards, hugging the shop fronts and terraced houses. In the darkness, they could just make out the top of the hill against the night sky as it levelled off. The sound of the striding machine was distant. It was heading towards Kent, away from the dead city.

"It has passed the point we are making for and is moving on," muttered Harry.

This was a moment of hopeful excitement. They had almost reached their goal. The sewer manhole was only a short distance away. Excited, they moved on, still using the shops and the doorways for cover. They crept along up the last part of the rising road, stopping in a doorway to check before making for the next section of concealment. Soon, much to everyone's delight, the old brewery was in sight.

Sammy was flushed with excitement. "That's close to the manhole entrance. We're almost home and dry."

"Hush," said Sister Ciara. "What's that noise?"

Everyone suddenly froze. There was a snarling sound in the darkness. Fear yanked at Sammy's stomach. Slowly, he turned to see where the growling was coming from. His revolver was out and ready to fire. Again, they heard the snarling noise.

"There!" whispered Harry pointing.

A vicious looking dog growled nervously from the dark recess of a shop doorway. Foam dribbled from bared teeth. Petrified eyes glared from the corner of the shop's dark alcove.

"It's that same sick dog we saw yesterday morning," muttered Sammy. "The one that walked out of the brewery."

Now it looked even more dishevelled, plagued to an even greater intensity. The others realised Sammy was right. The very hound Sister Ciara suspected of carrying rabies. Now there was no doubt. Each of them froze, Immobile with fear. The hideous and wretched animal was growling and scared. All at the same time. The wide red-rimmed eyes conveyed terror. Its panic-stricken fear was of a magnitude they could only guess at.

"Stand still," said Harry.

"We must back away slowly," advised Sister Ciara. "The mutt is beyond any type of reason, Harry."

Sammy fell in beside Sister Ciara and slowly moved backwards with his gun raised. He whispered. "Look at the thing's bulging eyes."

"I know, Sammy," whispered Sister Ciara.

"They look as though they are going to explode."

The dog's terrified eyes burned with delirious fever. They were insane eyes, accompanied with growling and frothing teeth. White spume and fangs shone in the gloom. The animal clearly wanted to back away, but it was cornered. It was trying to press itself into the corner of the shop doorway. As though it could simply wish the wall and glass away. The mutt just wanted to be gone. It clearly perceived the people before its meagre sanctuary as a threat.

"Just back away," Sister Ciara repeated.

At that moment the dog seemed to stagger forward from the doorway. The demented animal was moving towards Sister Ciara. Snarling and growling a new look of intended attack. The creature had a clear weakness of the hind legs. The animal was unable to walk in a straight line. It swayed sideways and kept snarling as the white froth fell from its open jaws. The petrified eyes that were focused on the old nun.

Harry stood in front of Sister Ciara defensively as the crazed mutt staggered forwards. The infected beast somehow managed to leap on its inadequate hind legs. Its rabid teeth sank into Harry's arm.

The old convict screamed out. "You bastard!"

He smashed the butt of his rifle into the incensed brute's snout. The demented animal yelped and fell away, but only for a moment. It resumed its infectious attack with increased snarling fervour. The beast shot forwards at Harry, diseased teeth ripping into the old convict's shin. One vicious bite after another. A frenzy of snapping fangs tearing at Harry's flesh and bone. He screamed and roared as he went back at the demented animal. He had dropped his rifle and was now punching the dog, again and again. His bare fists pummelled away at the incensed yelping creature. He roared with further pain and anger as he fell clutching the mad dog. The man and dog were twisting and turning in hideous, rolling conflict. Amid the struggling melee, Harry managed to stand. He now had the dog by the scruff of the neck in one hand. The other grabbed the left hind quarter and lifted the twisting dog up above his head, slinging it back into the shop doorway with ferocious force. The animal was clearly winded by the impact as it staggered to regain its frenzied wits.

Two shots from Sammy's revolver ripped through the vague light of dawn. The dog yelped as each shot entered its rabid body. It fell on its side, dying and bleeding.

"My God," muttered Sister Ciara. "It's rabid. The bloody dog has rabies!"

Harry looked at his bleeding arms and leg. The dog had torn into his flesh in several places. Now his arm was throbbing. No doubt his heart was pumping the blood around his body, spreading the infection throughout.

Then the distant fighting machine let out its menacing call. *"Argh-loo..."*

"The Martians," gasped Sammy. "They must have heard my gunshots. I think the bloody thing is coming back."

All three gasped in fear. In the distance, they saw the fighting machine halt. It was well over a mile away, amid a cluster of trees. Then the giant edifice slowly turned. The green porthole twisted in to view. The array of small lights below the undercarriage glimmered like perverse eyes. Dim rays of morning sun began to break the eastern horizon. The faint lustre stroked the body trunk of the machine. Then the tripod took the first step back towards the London fringe, and made directly for them.

CHAPTER 11

THE FINAL RECKONING

"Quick Sammy, I want you to make for the derelict buildings over there. Where all the rubble is. The manhole cover is there. Do you remember?"

"Yes, Sister," replied Sammy. "Are you and Harry coming too?"

Sister Ciara pushed the boy towards the houses as she took off her duffel bag. "Take both the bags. As quick as possible Sammy. We need you to go now!"

"But Sister Ciara —".

"Not now Sammy, please. There's a good boy. Get the medicines to the manhole cover. Get them into the tunnels. Please Sammy. No arguments."

The boy put his revolver in the waistband of his trousers and picked up each of the duffel bags. He ran towards the mound of broken bricks.

He was relieved to see the manhole cover from the previous morning was still slightly raised, because of the slate they had left in the rim. He was able to get the duffel bags down into the safety of the sewers. He would not argue with Sister Ciara. He knew how important the medicines could be.

Sister Ciara turned to the injured convict. She put a hand around his waist and his arm over her shoulder.

"Come on, Harry. We need to get to the house there. The one where Sammy hid yesterday while we waited for the Martian to come. If that machine has seen us, I want it to search this house. I want it to see us going in. It must be led away from Sammy and the manhole cover. The creature's interest might be taken by the alien we shot yesterday." She nodded her head towards the dead Martian she had shot the previous morning. It was lying next to the smaller dormant fighting machine. "All these little things could have a diversionary influence."

Harry staggered forward, limping on his injured leg and grimacing at his throbbing and bleeding arm. "What's a diversionary influence?" Again he grimaced. He knew the dog bites were fatal. He allowed Sister Ciara to lead him into the building. Here they could access their new dire circumstance.

"A diversionary influence means we could put something interesting in front of the Martian and take the opportunity to be away while it is busy looking at the dead Martian. One of their own." Sister Ciara replied.

"I see," added Harry. "It would use its feeler things to search this place if it saw us come in here."

"I know, Harry. That is what I'm counting on."

"Well, that's all right if it gets me. My blood is rabid. I'm dead already Sister. We both know this. You get to Sammy. Go with the boy."

She shook her head. "I dare not, Harry. I do not want the machine to see the manhole cover. It may have already seen Sammy go there. I want it to know we are here. I want it to see the dead Martian from yesterday. I want as many distractions as possible away from Sammy. My going to Sammy's position might add attention to the manhole cover. That is something we do not want."

In the distance they could hear the approach of the Martian machine.

"It's returning to the outskirts of the city," muttered Sister Ciara. She was clearly anxious.

"The thing knows we are here." Harry gasped as he lent against the front room wall. His throbbing arm was getting worse.

"The creatures' interest have been awakened by the shots that killed the rabid dog. This is such horrendous bad fortune, Harry. We were all but there."

"Well, Sister. Let's hope Sammy is home and dry. He's a cheeky little sod, but basically a good boy."

He sighed as he examined his haemorrhaging and throbbing arm, then looked out of the window. In the morning radiance he took another look at the dead Martian corpse from the previous day. He glanced up at the dormant smaller fighting machine. It was just standing there, a derelict monument because of the death of its Martian navigator.

The old convict winced again. More pain was raking his arm and leg. He could feel his pulse quicken, increased palpitating that informed him of his impending demise. The thought of rabies breaking down what little sanity he had left was horrendous. He breathed in the cold air of dawn. He wanted to supress the dread. He wanted to charge at the anxiety and scream it down. But he also wanted to be rational. He took another deep breath and composed himself. It was still a splendid morning, despite the ruined city. The world was still wonderful, despite the approach of the thunderous foot falls. The world was glorious, even though the sound of the giant Martian contraption was growing louder and louder.

"This is my redemption moment, Sister Ciara," Harry panted.

Sister Ciara had tears in her eyes. "Harry, this is not —".

"No, Sister. No more talk. I'm going to lead that machine away. When I do, you must get to Sammy. Get down the manhole cover and into the tunnels. You and the boy must get away."

"All three of us need to get to the sewer sanctuary, Harry. You must come too. But we do need to divert the Martians."

"Sister Ciara, I am finished. The rabies must be in me. Right now, I can feel my pulse spreading the infection. I'm an ignorant man, Sister. But I understand what is going to happen to me. Let the Martian have its fill."

Sister Ciara was fighting back the tears. She was a pragmatic, often hard, lady. But this was remorse on an intensity she had not expected. "Oh, Harry," she sighed apologetically.

He smiled. "Look out there. The very machine you put two bullets through. The green film of the Martian machine's porthole is not strong enough to stop your elephant gun's bullets, Sister Ciara. You said you would keep the knowledge in case it might be useful. That was yesterday morning. Look!" He nodded to the east. "It's almost dawn. The following morning, Sister. Take that knowledge back to the sewer sanctuary now."

"No one can ask this of you, Harry. It might not work." Sister Ciara knew it was a pointless conversation and she suddenly stopped her attempt at reason. The simple man was right.

Harry looked out the window at Sammy by the manhole cover. "The boy has put the medicine bags into the manhole. Soon he'll be in the sewer network. He must get the medicines to the sewer hospital. I will buy us time and my redemption. I am not committing suicide, Sister Ciara. I'm already dead. I will suffer from the rabies infection soon. I'll die anyway. This is martyrdom."

The bellowing call of the Martian tripod roared out over the London basin. Then the machine came into view above the rooftops. The underneath of the huge tripod's light apparatus and its symmetrical indentations glowed in the dawn light. It was awesome to behold at such close quarters – a huge tripod that was larger than the immobile machine close by. It stopped amid the ruins, outside the derelict house in which they were hiding.

Sister Ciara noted Harry's concern as he looked out of the window towards the brick rubble where the manhole cover was. Sammy had put the duffel bags down, but had panicked upon the tripod's arrival. He had not got down the manhole but had scampered behind a pile of debris and beneath some boarding.

The Martians inside their colossal vehicle had not noticed the boy. The giant machine's mechanisms appeared to be intent on its own examination. The familiar testing device with the green beam swept over the empty smaller Martian machine. The testing appliance ran for a few seconds and then switched off. Its conclusion was probably established by the sight of the dead Martian close by. One of the machine's mechanical feelers swept over the dead alien.

There followed another ear-splitting bellow from the machine, like a giant beast lamenting a dead pup. The noise shook the ground. Sister Ciara gulped nervously when she saw Sammy scuttle further under the debris where he was hiding. If the giant contraption turned and looked down, the boy might be instantly spotted.

This was the moment Harry chose to run out of the building. He limped awkwardly along the cobbled road. The machine did not seem to be aware of him at first. Harry staggered back towards the discarded rifle he had dropped when fighting the dog. In great pain, he managed to bend down and grab the Lee-Enfield. He struggled to lift it with his blood-soaked arm, and somehow he managed it. Cumbersomely, he lifted the rifle and took aim. His arm was shaking with the effort. Then the old convict let loose with two rounds. Both pinged against the body casing of the Martian machine. For a moment there was stunned silence. It was as though the world had stopped in surprise. The glorious dawn was progressing in earnest and in that small bubble of quiet, Harry smiled. The huge trunk grated and squeaked as it slowly rotated. The green porthole came around and stared down at him. The condemned prisoner saw the alien silhouette behind the green, murky resin. The Martian occupants had finally come upon a scarce human. A precious food commodity.

Harry grunted with a sigh of satisfaction. He turned and started to stagger towards the smaller machine, acting as bait. Limping away from the house and the manhole cover, tempting the active machine to commit to the chase. Cheekily, he staggered between the empty tripod's legs and across the larger active fighting machine's green window canopy. The screen had been turning with the trunk, following the old convict's movements. The condemned man stopped before the dead Martian. He fired a third shot into the alien corpse. The loud bang of the gun echoed in the rising dawn. Perhaps he hoped to irritate the Martians, further tempt them to commit to the chase. The old man turned back to face the active fighting machine with a defiant grin.

"We killed one of your mates," he roared and then started to laugh. "Come on then, me ole mucker! What ya waiting for?"

The dawn was beginning to send shafts of light through the diminishing gloom. He noticed the old

Pears soap advertisement board that Sister Ciara had put two bullet holes through. He lurched towards it and awkwardly picked the board up. "We got a nice little surprise for you," he laughed. He looked at the board with the two bullet holes in it. He caught a glimpse of Sister Ciara staring out of the house window at him. Her usual hard stare was gone. Now it was a face of pity and gratitude. He turned away from the nun's gaze and threw the board down, still clutching his rifle in the other hand.

"So it ends here," he laughed. "The Martians return in their giant vehicle because of the gun shots spent on a rabid dog. A nice bit of salt and pepper for ya."

Now, the Martian contraption was clearly focused upon the old man. One way or another, he would destroy the two Martians in the fighting machine.

"You ugly brutes are doomed!" He laughed hysterically.

The machine's mechanical joints began to creak. As though in protest. The giant device's head lowered slightly to observe the small man. Harry tried to lift his rifle for another shot at the green porthole, but his throbbing arm made the action too difficult. His blood-stained hand gripped the bolt but it was too painful to pull the mechanism back.

He cursed as a huge feeler from the fighting machine shot forward and smacked the rifle from his grasp. It clattered across the cobblestones. Shaken by the impact, Harry quickly pulled himself together and looked up at the green aperture.

"Come on then. Get on with it," he shouted.

Nervously, he forced himself to stand still, a condemned being awaiting sentence. The silhouette of a strange body form moved on the other side of the green viewer. He could make out the appendages. Then he became aware of the mechanical tentacles on the outside. One came down and slithered about his waist. The old convict looked up and started to laugh. He continued to chuckle as the appendage lifted him high into the air. There was a moment of nervous exhilaration. High in the air, he saw the daybreak over the eastern horizon and felt spiritually elated. Then another surge of excitement inflated his courage as he dangled there. It was further consolation as he recognised the tiny distant figure of Sister Ciara emerge from the house. Harry looked down at the nun. He watched as she made her way across the road. The Martians in their machine were oblivious of her. Little Sammy was looking up from the boarding and debris by the manhole cover. His two medicine bags had gone, thankfully, down the sewer. The boy would soon be home and dry, along with the much-needed medicine. The Martians had missed the two healthy specimens. Now they would feed from his infected blood. He laughed some more as the morning sun's rays burst over the horizon with increased brilliance. The heavenly beams bathed him. An anointment of light that made him feel spiritual and clean. He dropped his bloodied arms, held out his open palms in pious supplication. He remembered the old Gregorian chants he had once heard as a child in a cathedral or church. Harry could hear those same heavenly chants in his head as he dangled there, prepared for martyrdom.

"The angels are coming for me," he called with spiritual enthusiasm. His eyes were watering with the joy of deliverance as the sun broke above the eastern horizon. The Lord's Prayer – he did not know the exact words but had some idea. He began to call them out.

"Deliverance from evil," he roared and then continued. "For you are the kingdom and the power and the glory for ever. Amen."

The first barbed feeler struck into his left shoulder. He felt the injection of a liquid and then groaned as the enzyme raked through his body. He began to tremble and was soon in throes of, what looked like, an epileptic fit. He convulsed, choked and shook violently. His entire body from head to foot was shuddering spasmodically. Finally, he vomited a hideous green bile. A second barb shot down and punctured his right shoulder. His blood was instantly being drained and the brown irises of his eyes vanished upwards as though peering into his inner skull. Just the demented whites of the lower sclera remained. He hung there limply, as his life was sucked out of him.

Inside, the doomed Martians would be ingesting his contaminated blood.

Sammy could not bring himself to drop into the dark sanctuary. The manhole cover was open but he could not leave Sister Ciara. Not yet. He crawled from beneath the boarding as he saw the giant contraption's trunk turn. The green porthole was looking away, towards the London basin. There was a pile of debris that rose to the wall of a destroyed building, cover from which he could observe. He knew Sister Ciara would be angry with him, but he could not go. The concerned youngster had caught sight of the nun when she left the house and made for the derelict brewery's open gates. He scampered up the incline of bricks towards an opening in the broken wall. Attaining an advantage of height, he caught a second glimpse of Sister Ciara.

The determined old nun clutched the huge hunting rifle as she made purposeful strides. Her black habit fluttered in the morning light. She was an avenging saint, ready to take on this abomination to God. Sister Ciara looked the complete opposite of divine duty. But then again, an acceptable, though twisted, confirmation. The crisscross bullet belt added to the ominous sense of a holy confrontation soon to come. She was composed, with a devoted sense of purpose. She vanished upon entering the brewery gates close to the chimney stack.

Sammy knew Sister Ciara would want the height. He crossed himself the way the sisters of the sewer sanctuary had taught him. Then he turned his attention to the fighting machine. He watched in petrified awe as Harry's limp body dangled in the grip of one of the Martian machine's feelers. The old man was dead. The boy felt a pang of dread and deep disappointment. Harry had been a very brave man, a hero to the last. He would be in Heaven now. He had left the world where bad people were good and good people learnt to be bad.

"God be with you, Harry," muttered Sammy, and he crossed himself again.

The machine flicked its tentacle up like a whip. It cast Harry's used body away. The limp corpse smashed into a building wall and dropped lifeless to the ground, deformed and twisted – one more body among the millions throughout the streets of London.

The machine stepped forward one giant pace. It stood above the building where Harry and Sister Ciara had been hiding. The machine's feelers smashed through the upstairs window while another went down and through the front door. The whole place was empty but the Martians clearly did not know this. The fruitless search continued for a few minutes and then the tentacles came out. The fighting machine stood legs astride at full height, towering into the dawn sky, while its whirring mechanics continued to hum away. Slowly, its body trunk revolved. The green orb of the porthole swept a view of the London basin again. As the revolving trunk continued to turn, the luminous green aperture came into the view of the brewery complex. It would be exposed to the chimney stack. Sammy gasped with dread and excitement. Sister Ciara had made for the compound. The mad nun was going to try and do the same thing as she had the previous morning. But the Martian had left its machine then. It had been exposed. This fighting machine contained two Martians. It was bigger and they were inside a huge vehicle. Then he remembered the Pears soap advert boarding.

"Oh no Sister Ciara, no! Please don't be trying what I think you are going to do," he whispered to himself.

CHAPTER 12

THE FINAL ACT

Sister Ciara had entered the work yard and quickly made her way up the gantry steps. She walked briskly along the balcony of the upper complex wall, her boots stamping upon the gantry. Her black habit flapped in the dawn breeze as she looked down and checked the loaded rifle she firmly held. Satisfied, she took one reassuring grasp of the crucifix hanging just below her dirty, white scapular and stopped. It was for a split second as she made her commitment to the Almighty. Then she made the sign of the cross and continued with forthright resolve. Gritting her teeth as she approached the chimney stack, the lady of the cloth was a package of ultimate dedication. The children of the sewer sanctuary referred to her as *the mad nun with the gun,* and this nun had a task to complete – to visit violence upon hideous demons from another world.

Sister Ciara reached the next steel ladder, rungs affixed to the brickwork of the smokestack. As she strapped the rifle behind her shoulder she realised the vulnerable sensation of having the rifle out of her grip. She had carried the weapon devotedly throughout the mission. It was almost distressing, but she had to climb the ladder unhindered. Nimbly, the warrior nun scaled to the upper circular gantry. It was midway up the chimney stack and the position of the upper gantry represented an advantageous height gain. Sister Ciara smiled wickedly, for the remarkable gantry was a sight to behold. It surrounded the entire curved structure. It would not equal the height of the Martian vehicle, but it would be better for nearing such elevation. Perhaps between half and two-thirds of the machine's height. The brewery was also slightly up hill on higher ground than the huge alien contraption. It all aided the nun in her daring quest. The killing shot she intended to make would still require an upward trajectory, but not extreme.

Sister Ciara used the cover of the chimney while walking around the circular platform. She slowed down when she realised the bend of the wall would allow her a glimpse of the machine's new position. At such a height, the bluster of wind was stronger and her habit fluttered robustly. Yet she paid little attention to such matters. Instead, she unslung her rifle and felt the calming effect of its sublime power. The thought of the high velocity bullets caused an exhilarating adrenalin rush. The wicked power of such projectiles had often been explained by the late Sir Fotheringhay Beecham. Now such malevolence could be put to more Godly use.

The colossal alien edifice had come clearly into view as she cautiously peered around the curve of the brick stack. This was the position that Sister Ciara chose as her killing spot. Carefully, she knelt down on one leg. She was now exposed, but the framework of the rail offered some concealment. The monster was before and above her, a giant humming contraption alive with hidden controls. Almost like the sound of a textile factory – more machines of human subjugation, sounds she had learnt to loath throughout her caring career. Now she could be a Luddite, with a clear conscious.

Sister Ciara pondered the moment and event before her. She was a small, human woman before a grotesque celestial being – a Nephilim biblical creature from beyond the time of the Deluge. Then she remembered the Greek tales. Could she become an Argonaut? Was the chimney stack her Argo? Was the fighting machine her Talos?

No! She shook her head and returned to reality. This was real. This was an alien machine, controlled by ugly Martian beings. She made one more quick check of her faithful hunting rifle, then waited for the opportunity that would surely present itself – the moment she knew would come if she knelt there patiently. The defiant barrel of the elephant gun was resting on the horizontal bar of the gantry guard rail. One eye closed, while her aiming eye remained fixed along the gun's sights. She was waiting for the green orb – the aperture on the fighting machine's revolving turret, the weak spot of the Martian machine.

It came into view, and the turning contraption stopped. A loud clunk then everything was locked down and turned off. At that moment all went still and quiet. There was nothing but an eerie silence that seemed to want to scream. It was almost as though the occupants inside the alien vehicle had spotted her. Sister Ciara held her breath. The green porthole with its gelatine film cover was sitting snuggly in her gun sight. Her finger gently squeezed the final stage of the trigger. The powerful gun loudly cracked out.

A shot ripped out in the silence of the morning light. The avenging nun rode the kick back with well-trained ability, a skill mastered from her days at Sir Fotheringhay Beecham's charitable fund-raising events. The high-powered projectile zipped upwards across the morning air and the cobbled road. It smacked into the green congealed film of the porthole viewer. The shadowed silhouette on the other side of the surveillance dock jolted, with a violent and telling impact. The distorted Martian figure fell away from the green observation port. Then a second lurid profile replaced the fallen outline. The appendages inside the machine appeared to splay in various directions as though taking over the controls. The ruptured green resin smoothed over the puncture of the bullet hole.

"*Arghloo!*"

The bellow of the Martian war cry was like a gigantic horn. The outer mechanical feeler holding the heat-ray device lifted. Sister Ciara scrambled back behind the brickwork of the chimney stack as the whirl of the alien gun began to charge up. A *whoosh* followed as a javelin of burning light tore out across the road and sliced through the brick stack. Sister Ciara had instinctively thrown herself to the floor of the gantry. The light tore through the brickwork above her. She rolled onto her back to see the huge upper funnel toppling. Cascading bricks began to list above her.

"Talos is throwing rocks," she gasped.

The whole thing was about to collapse. With no time to lose, and her petty indulgence put aside,

Sister Ciara scampered to her feet. Clutching her rifle, she ran to the gantry ladder. She had taken barely a few steps down when instinctively she let her grip go. It was another moment when time seemed to stand still. The entire structure was moving away from her. She calmly stepped away from the departing metal ladder rungs out into the air. The moment was distinctly absorbed. There was time to observe all that was happening in lingering split seconds. Still she clutched her powerful hunting rifle amid the monumental and surreal instant. She seemed to be suspended in the mid-air and watched the entire brick column fall away from her.

Instinctively, she knew it had been necessary. Then she had the sensation of dropping down about fifteen feet towards the lower metal platform that ran the length of the brewery wall. It was a dream-like descent as the middle-aged nun calmly watched the gantry come up to meet her dusty black boots.

Sister Ciara landed hard but well. Her glasses had fallen off and clattered a few feet away. The expected impact was kinder than anticipated. She rolled with the way instilled from her youth, and taught in her adult years. She had been fond of gymnastic classes. She had managed to keep the big rifle firmly in her clutches. She believed that the all-knowing and all-seeing entity was helping her ride the dramatic storm of events. Like a sprightly young woman, she recovered and stood. Her mind was racing ahead, and notions quickly fell into order. Had she really ridden such a fall, or was she fuelled by her pulsating adrenalin rush? She thanked the Lord and made the sign of the cross. There was no injury. Not even a twisted ankle. She moved forward, clutched her unappealing spectacles and pushed them back on. She was just in time to watch the entire brick chimney stack crash across the opposite side of the work compound like a shattered serpent. It was a sight of destruction to behold. Dust and smoke billowed up, engulfing her as she forced her attention from the spectacle. Quickly, the old nun made haste for the other gantry steps further along the platform. Her wrinkled hands pulled the bolt of the rifle back. Her long skinny fingers removed a slender bullet from the ammunition belt. With practised ease the projectile was inserted into the rifle and the bolt rammed back in place. Another shot was ready and waiting.

Her habit was turning grey as she moved through the billowing brick dust – an avenging angel pacing through the cloud, slayer of Martians. She had one more shot to go for, one more Martian to kill. It could not move away from the green viewer. It would need to stand by the vulnerable spot to work its vehicle.

Again she heard the whirring of the heat gun. Instinctively, she fell forward, face down on the deck of the platform. The heat ray ripped across the wall, a line of piped laser fire cutting through the compound's brickwork like a hot sword through butter. Once again, the line of heat passed above her body as bricks and dust spewed over and about her. She held her hand against her mouth to stop the choking dirt. She felt the walkway construction giving way ahead of her. The platform came to a clattering halt at a gradient of around thirty degrees. Her elephant gun fell from her grasp, slid down onto the billowing brick powder. Desperately, she crawled down through the choking debris, and there she grabbed her prized rifle. She rolled over on to her back to face the loud humming sound of the alien machine. Its huge trunk appeared over the broken wall of the brewery. The overpowering whirl of its mechanics vibrated from within the capsule. *More factory sounds, more machine subjugation.* The joints of the monstrosity creaked and groaned as the colossal trunk bent down, like the giant head of mythical Talos. The vile green window was before her, just feet away, illuminating through the dust. The shadowy Martian silhouette moved on the other side of the shimmering hazy green membrane. The heat gun above the trunk was pointing down at her. Suddenly, the high-pitched whizz of the apparatus began to charge. It would hit a high point, and then spew a jet of concentrated heat in a second.

But Sister Ciara's rifle was already raised, the butt was jammed against her shoulder. One eye was closed, while the other stared through the dusty lens of her spectacles, fixed upon the shadow beyond the green porthole. Her finger squeezed the trigger just as the Martian device reached a crescendo.

The rifle shot ripped out and smashed through the gelatine view port. Sister Ciara did not see the stricken shadow jolt as the projectile smashed into it. Nor the flaming heat ray that emitted from the gun above her.

CHAPTER 13

ON WITH THE MISSION

S ammy had witnessed it all, this new version of
David and Goliath. He had watched the giant
machine bend over the smashed wall. He heard the
gun shot. He knew she had been alive all during the
collapse of the chimney stack.

Now it was over. Sister Ciara's death had rocked
him. There could be no mistake. The flashing
light of the heat ray had shot down with powerful
force a split second after the rifle shot. It was obvious the Martian was killed as the heat-ray apparatus smashed down into the debris where the
shot came from. All the tripod's arms dropped,
smashing limply upon the surrounding rubble.
The trunk of the machine clicked into a strange,
automated motion, moving up and backwards
before dropping. Another dead fighting machine,

now surrounded by the destruction and dust of the brewery.

Panic stricken; Sammy called out for her. "Sister Ciara! Sister Ciara!"

He ran across the debris-laden street and scrambled up the pile of bricks beside the machine. At the top he looked over the wrecked factory wall. Perhaps he hoped that somehow Sister Ciara had survived.

"Heroes always find a way," he told himself. "They don't get killed."

Just for a moment he clung to hope. Below, where the heat ray had shot down, Sammy saw the smouldering pile. Black ash around a black smoking skeletal frame. Then hope was dashed.

He screamed out. "No!" Then he looked to the huge monstrosity and screamed. "No!" He looked up to Heaven and was about to berate God, but he held back. Sister Ciara would never want that.

He turned away from the scene and fought back tears. The boy looked about at the immediate destruction and the two derelict devices they had immobilised over the last twenty-four hours. He thought of the others the group had stopped during the mission. They were somewhere out across the panorama of the ruined metropolis, among the many other immobile tripods that littered the landscape. He viewed every giant fighting machine with contempt and hatred. Then he stood up on the rubble and gritted his teeth in triumphant as he turned his attention back to the tripod before him. More food inside the container for the carrion and crows. Sister Ciara had slaughtered Martians again and again. Now there stood another spent machine. Another one to stand alongside the many vanquished – sterile and defeated amid the rising brick dust. Sister Ciara had done it. The old nun had killed two more Martians, this time at the cost of her own life. Just twenty minutes ago, all three of them thought they were home and dry. Now, it was just him. Why had he survived? Why had God taken Sister Ciara and Harry? The boy began to sob as he forced himself down the rubble and back towards the manhole.

"Everything can change on the turn of a six-pence," he thought.

He must get to the manhole cover. He would do so right away. Sister Ciara would be very cross with him if he did not do as instructed.

CHAPTER 14

THE PRIORESS OUTSIDE
THE SEWER SANCTUARY

"We are not going to throw them in the park area like the others, are we, Sister Cathleen?" Sammy looked concerned and agitated.

The Prioress looked down at the boy.

"No Sammy. We will make Sister Ciara and Harry a very special case. We will bury them straight away. All the other poor souls will be given a proper resting place when this Martian problem is finally over. And it will be soon. I'm doing this for you, because you have done a great service for our sewer sanctuary. Sister Ciara and Harry have made the ultimate sacrifice to help us."

"It was not suicide, Sister Cathleen. Sister Ciara fought until the very end, with every last part of her."

The Prioress leaned down and gently squeezed Sammy's arm. "I know Sammy. Sister Ciara and Harry fought all the way."

"Harry says he was in Purgatory after his sentence of hanging. He thought he might have redeemed himself and can now go to Heaven."

"I am sure he has redeemed himself. I think we will all see him again in Heaven. I will write a letter to the Pope concerning Harry. I'm certain the Pope would read such a letter. I think the Pope would pray for Harry. He will be a special case, young man."

"How do you get to make special cases, Sister Cathleen?"

"Well, I have to make decisions and exceptions from time to time." The Prioress was anxious to put the boy's troubles to rest. He had done very well and been exceptionally brave. He was a brash and saucy young urchin, but a rogue that people might willingly warm to. She began to understand why Sister Ciara had liked the lovable rascal.

"Do people listen to you a lot, Sister Cathleen?" he watched as the stretcher bearers awkwardly tried to descend the rubble of the destroyed factory complex. They were carrying the remains of Sister Ciara beneath a blanket cover.

"Well, sometimes they do, Sammy. I think we will get a sympathetic ear from most Godly people after what we have been through."

Sammy looked thoughtful. "So if you wrote a letter to the Pope he would read it. And because you have done God's work here in this Purgatory of Earth, you might get a more symp..." he lingered on the word.

"Sympathetic?" advised the Prioress.

"Yes the word you just used. The Pope would give your letter sympathetic, which is something good?"

The Prioress smiled. "Yes Sammy. I believe the Pope might give sympathetic attention to my letter of request."

"The Pope can make saints, can't he Sister Cathleen?"

The Prioress frowned. "Well, yes. A Pope can do things like that."

"Can you ask the Pope to be sympathetic and make Sister Ciara a saint?"

"You want me to ask the Pope to make Sister Ciara a saint?"

"Yeah," replied Sammy. "She could be Saint Ciara. Our Lady of Martian Slayers."

The Prioress was astounded by the request. Sammy was a boy. What would a boy know of such things? What would a most un-Catholic rascal know of saints?

"I don't think..."

The Prioress stopped and thought about the request. She looked into the face of the pleasingly cheeky young urchin. Then the tall Prioress bent down. "I'll tell you what I will do, Sammy. I'll write two letters. One for Harry's absolution. For I know he asked such things and did confess for forgiveness of his wrongdoing. I will also ask if the Pope would consider a boy's request to make Sister Ciara a saint. I do not think it will be granted. But I will try. Would you like me to do that?"

Sammy smiled. "Yes, Sister Cathleen. I would like that very much."

The Prioress stood up as the stretcher bearers walk past with the covered bones of Sister Ciara.

"Our Lady of Martian Slayers."

She sighed, and again, looked down at the street urchin. "We'll have to return to the sewer sanctuary now. But I do not think it will be for too much longer, young man."

They turned and made their way back to the pile of debris near the manhole cover. Two armed men were standing close by.